# ABOUT THE BOOK

Natalya Stravinsky and her boisterous Russian family are on the hunt for a champion to protect Nat from the ultimate threat. Not long after a harrowing confrontation with one of the goddess Diana's hellhounds, Nat's family makes the difficult decision to leave South Tom's River New Jersey to find an enchanted seed capable of summoning a great champion: a dragon.

But the seed comes at a steep price: Nat must uncover a mysterious killer who's been hunting innocent supernaturals in a hidden forest community. With a vengeful goddess and her relentless hounds on her trail, Nat must summon her inner strength in order to apprehend the killer, and summon the dragon before she becomes one of Diana's hunting hounds for all eternity.

# FEROCIOUS FLEA MARKET DRAGONS

A Flea Market Magic Novel

NEW YORK TIMES BESTSELLING AUTHOR

## SHAWNTELLE MADISON

VALKYRIE
RISING
PRESS

Whoever invented slushies deserved a snazzy national award. On the hottest days, those things tasted like heaven. Especially after the first brain freeze-inducing sip. Once the drink melts, you've got even more to enjoy. A win-win, I say.

My ten-month-old niece, Sveta, squirmed and grinned in her car seat with red-stained lips. She'd gobbled up every spoonful I gave her. Grandma Lasovskaya, Sveta, and I sat in the backseat while Mom and Karey sat in the front.

"Oh, Natalya, she's never gonna sleep tonight," my sister-in-law Karey grumbled from the driver's seat. "Did she drink the whole thing?"

"You're with family," my mom said firmly from the passenger seat. "Don't worry. Her *deduska* and *babushka* will mind our sweet baby."

"I'm serious about my auntie duties." I covertly slid Sveta another cracker. "If I'm not spoiling my *printsessa*, I'm not doing it right."

Grandma grinned with approval.

It was moments like these—seeing Sveta grin at me—that

made me forget about the proverbial asteroid hurling in my direction. The mellow pop music from the radio and the pleasant Maine breeze through the rolled-down windows wouldn't stop the goddess Diana from hunting me down with her hellhounds.

Two months ago, I'd tangled with a creepy creature called the Basilisk King. He'd set loose a bunch of basilisks back home. To capture him, I'd gotten close to the goddess's hunting grounds north of town and lured him there. Diana snatched not only the Basilisk King, but me too. Thanks to Karey's aunt Mevelyn, I returned home and the wood nymph stayed in my place. I thought I was free and clear, but the goddess's promises to come for me again were true.

Sveta's sticky fingers reached for another cracker, drawing me away from my dark thoughts.

The sign down the road read, "Welcome to Stitchings!" Underneath that, the population boasted three hundred. This was a true small town. We'd finally made it to our haven—until we had to make a run for it again.

After escaping South Toms River due a hellhound's arrival, my family had escaped to the north. We drove up to Massachusetts, then rested overnight before the final push to Maine.

Karey pulled into the gravel parking lot in front of Stitchings' only grocery store. Like most small towns, the place also served as the liquor store and garden supply depot. I wouldn't be surprised if they sold bait too. Their spot was ideal. Moosehead Lake was nestled right next to the store and a marina. At this time of the day—mid-morning on a Saturday—tourists docked and took out pontoons for a pleasant late July outing.

The Stravinskys, though, wouldn't be boating this week. We were leaving as soon as I snagged the seed Grandma had told us about. To be honest, I wasn't sure if all that research

Mom and Grandma had undertaken was true, but if she believed there was a shop that sold seeds capable of summoning a champion, I had to try to find the place.

As I lifted Sveta out of the car seat, I couldn't help but notice we only had one other car with us. Aunt Vera and Aunt Olga pulled into the next spot, but Uncle Boris's van and Thorn's SUV were missing. Dad had tagged along with them as they'd headed south to throw the hellhound off our trail.

My phone practically nipped at me from my jeans pocket. Anything could go wrong and my mate and family would get caught in the middle. To keep my twitchy fingers from calling Thorn, I rained kisses on my niece's forehead instead. Sveta giggled and my fast-beating heart steadied briefly.

As Aunt Olga and my two teenaged cousins got out of the car, Karey headed over to a shorter evergreen. She briefly ran her fingers along the pointy leaves, then she returned to join us. The nymph probably used her magic for a quick conversation. My aunt Vera was the last to get out. She adjusted her snug knit skirt and drew up her black hair into a ponytail. It was far too hot for her European chic sensibilities.

We headed inside and the cool air fanned our faces.

"Very nice," Grandma Lasovskaya said in her soft-spoken voice.

"Did you get any intel from the tree?" I asked Karey as she grabbed a shopping cart. After wiping down a greasy spot on the cart handles with an antibacterial wipe, I placed Sveta in the child seat in the front.

"It's too soon to know anything," she replied. "I just let the tree know to pass along anything suspicious."

"Thanks. It's awesome to know every tree you've visited is now a gossip mill."

We shared a smiled before she added, "Oak and birch

trees are much chattier than the evergreens, but all trees are nosy, so we should learn a lot soon."

The air conditioner in the back of the store groaned louder than my father-in-law Farley's snores. I was surprised the place was cool.

The store itself was a cozy den of essentials, boasting only three aisles. My kind of place. There was even a bulletin board for community announcements. I'd asked Bill about adding one at my former workplace, The Bend of the River Flea Market, or The Bends as the locals called it, but he'd always put his foot down.

"Why should I give *free* advertising space for somebody else?" he'd grumbled. "Next thing ya know, we got pyramid scheme flyers all over the place."

At the time, I'd tried to explain we'd use the board like this store did. Anybody frequenting this place would see a traveling carnival was coming to Stitchings in two days.

Again, I *didn't* want to be here to check it out.

As we ambled past the shelves, I couldn't help but notice an unusually generous candy section in the back. The rows practically winked at me with their colorful wrappers and sweet promises. My eyes met with Sveta's and her round face lit up. Her tiny fingers reached out for a candy bar.

"Not today, sweetie," Karey said softly. "You still need to eat dinner."

Ah, but who could resist such temptation? After Karey wandered down the aisle with Grandma shuffling after, I snagged a Hershey's bar.

My regal, blonde-haired Aunt Olga nodded with approval as she observed the covert exchange. "Good choice."

"I think so too," I replied with a grin.

We neared the single fridge for beverages and a hulking freezer for meat as the soft strains of an old Hank Williams tune drifted from the radio. Mom scampered over with glee.

She'd already piled cans of vegetables, loaves of bread, and tubs of Rocky Road ice cream into the cart, but now she hurried over to grab the most important staple: meat.

"Do you want me to get another cart?" I asked, raising an eyebrow at the growing mountain of provisions.

She grinned at me, her blue eyes sparkling with excitement. "An army runs on its stomach," she reminded me. "It's been a long time since I've made a real fire pit and roasted our dinner. I can't wait for your dad to start digging."

I tried to smile, knowing Mom was trying to add normalcy to an unexpected trip.

Mom added, "I can't wait to teach Sveta how to make s'mores. We can even have hot dogs too." She stole a glance at Aunt Vera. "Her kids don't like hot dogs," she whispered. "Shame."

Aunt Vera heard every word and pursed her lips.

I chuckled, joining her as she rifled through the floor freezer for bulk meat. She examined the frozen packages and the look of concentration on her face never faltered.

"They've got plenty of mackerel and perch," I said, passing her a packet.

She sighed wistfully and her gaze grew distant for a moment. "You know, your dad and I used to fish at the marina when we first moved to South Toms River. Fyodor was horrible at it too. Couldn't catch a thing, but I loved how he tried to be cool about it. 'It's okay, Anna,' he'd say to me. I can take my pretty wife out to eat."

I smiled. "Well, at least he tried."

"He did." She stole a glance out the window—perhaps she hoped Dad had returned sooner than expected. "At least your husband can fish."

On the way to the register, Mom veered off to the back. Like any sneaky grandma, she grabbed another Hershey's bar and slipped it beneath the groceries.

At last, we made our way to the checkout, but there was no one behind the counter. Mom and I peered over the edge and were met with the sight of a wiry-haired fairy perched on a stool, her fingers nimbly knitting a tapestry of colorful threads. She didn't wear a glamour—which I didn't find unusual since she had a very human-like appearance. The short fairy wore a brightly colored peasant shirt and capri pants. The script on her name tag read "Patty."

"Done with your shopping, are you?" Patty inquired, her gaze meeting ours. With a jerk of her chin, the stool rose, bringing her to eye level with us.

"Do you have any lamb?" Mom asked. "Nice and lean?"

The fairy grinned. "Not today, dearie. Care for some deer? It's ten dollars a pound."

Mom hid her displeasure with a curt nod. "Not at that price. I'll tackle one of those on my own and put it in my pot."

I chuckled, knowing full well we bought half the meat in the freezer.

The clerk went through the cart to add up the items. She paused as she added the tubs of ice cream into a bag.

"My grandma likes ice cream."

"You plan to stay long? We normally don't have were-wolves come here—well, until recently, that is."

"Just for a spell. We needed a nice, quiet family trip," Mom said.

*Hopefully not too long of a spell*, I couldn't help but think.

Eight stuffed bags later, we wrapped up the purchase.

The fairy leaned in with the kind of excitement a human might reserve for juicy gossip. "Well, let me tell you folks about the troubles around here. About two months ago, it all began with a brownie, a cheeky little thing who fancied herself a mushroom forager."

I glanced at Mom. "What happened?"

"She owned the trading post just down the street. One night during the full moon, she left her shop—with the front door standing wide open—but she never returned."

Mom frowned. "That's terrible!"

Patty's expression turned somber. "Her family searched for days on end. My people, the fairy folk, found the poor thing washed up on the far shore of the lake." Her voice lowered as she stole a peek at Sveta. "Her throat had been torn out."

She kept going, probably unaware that Sveta repeated far worse after hearing Uncle Boris speak from a football field away. "It was a heartbreaking sight and that wasn't the end of it. A month ago, during the full moon, a sprite met a sinister fate as well."

I shuddered. Beside me, Karey's grip on the shopping cart tightened. Guess that nosy tree network hadn't told her about that.

"So, two disappearances," I said, "both ending in tragedy around the full moon. Does everyone suspect a nearby pack is involved?"

Patty nodded solemnly. "Yeah. Folks can't help but point fingers."

Grandma raised a shrewd eyebrow. "They always blame our people," she quipped in Russian.

The fairy slowly nodded. Guess she understood Russian. "The world can be quick to point fingers, my elder sister."

Patty's gaze shifted to Sveta. "Watch over the young one. This area is dangerous at night."

On the counter, I spotted a photo of Patty and her family. She had a husband and four kids, all grown and smiling through their human-like glamours. I hoped Patty's family would be careful around here.

"She'll be fine," I assured her. "Thanks for the warning."

As we gathered our bags and returned outside, the

somber mood followed us. I didn't expect every place we'd visit to be all sunshine and happy distractions, but I hadn't thought we'd find murderous werewolves.

Loading up the car, I cast a glance down the quiet street that stretched along the tranquil lake. We needed time to rest. I needed it most of all. The calm waters should've acted as balm to my worries, but I couldn't help but sense an undercurrent of unease around here, a reminder that danger, like a lurking shadow, could be just beyond the horizon.

Our two cars rumbled and rattled their way down the winding Maine country road as we ventured farther north of Stitchings. No one said a word, the fairy's news dampening the mood. Even Sveta said little and merely cuddled with her favorite stuffed animal.

Not long after we'd escaped town, Thorn called me.

"Where are you?" I didn't bother with hellos at this point.

"We're right outside of Stitchings," he replied over the sounds of Starship belting out "We Built This City" from the radio.

The weight on my shoulders briefly lifted. I smiled, knowing Uncle Boris had taken over the radio as usual. The man changed the radio station at every opportunity.

"Did you throw the hellhound off your trail?" I asked carefully.

"Don't worry," my dad said softly through the line. "We haven't done anything crazy." Even with the loud music, my father heard our conversation with his excellent werewolf hearing.

"We took your old clothes and put them on a train

heading into Canada," Thorn said. "Your brother checked the manifest and it's heading northwest to Manitoba."

"Wait. Wait. Did you and Alex put it on a passenger train?" I asked.

"Oh, no," Thorn said quickly. "It's a freight train transporting pipes and construction equipment for loggers."

"Is there any way to know if that thing took the bait?" I asked.

"Not really," Thorn said, "but I believe it'll work. Think of those bastards as pack animals. They track their prey until they corner them."

"It'll buy us some time, Natalya," Dad said. "Don't worry."

Since they were close, we wrapped up our phone call. Grandma reached over and patted my hand. "Everything will be well."

We didn't have to wait long before we reached a fork in the road, then a sharp left to a narrow gravel lane leading to our temporary sanctuary. The tires kicked up small clouds of dust and the gnats scattered. The serene countryside flitted past the window as sunlight danced through the leaves of the trees, casting shifting patterns on the road.

"Pretty," Grandma murmured.

Mom occasionally turned around from the passenger seat to glance at me with concern in her eyes, but I kept my expression steady. Perhaps my scent betrayed my true feelings. Beside me, Grandma hummed an old tune I'd heard often.

As we drew closer, anticipation filled the car. We'd made it. Two charming cabins came into view, nestled between the pines and facing a decent-sized pond. The water's surface shimmered like glass, reflecting the sky and the clouds drifting overhead.

The gravel road extended up to a small parking lot in front of the homes. Aunt Vera parked next to the second cabin, while Mom parked her car next to the first. It didn't take long for the older Stravinsky women to cluck like hens organizing a coop.

"You and your brother will share the bunk beds in the last bedroom," Aunt Vera barked out to her teenagers. My cousins slipped out of her minivan and stretched. Meanwhile, Aunt Olga admired the countryside.

"This is just like the first cabin I shared with my Pyotr." Grandma beamed up at the single-story structure.

"I wish I could've seen it, Mama," Aunt Olga said.

"Did you have dead flowers in front?" Aunt Vera asked dryly.

That got Grandma laughing as she shook her head.

The lady who owned the cabin said nothing about the dried husks poking out of the window planters or the moss-covered little stone gnomes guarding the front. Defiant weeds poked out of the gaps on the stone path leading up to the pond.

"How much did you pay for this place?" Mom asked me.

"Does it matter?" I replied. "I got a deal."

She shrugged. "Good point."

At this time of the year, cabins like these were snatched up for vacationing families, youth groups, and such. The lady I called last night from Massachusetts gushed with delight when I asked about availability. Now I knew why. The beautiful pond had a rickety-looking pier, its wooden planks weathered and off-kilter. A pair of discolored armchairs sat at the edge. One leaned to the side, daring a bold soul to take a seat.

Karey took Sveta out of the car. My niece made a beeline toward the water. Karey hurried after her. For the life of me, I never understood the death wish kids had with bodies of water. As a toddler pup, Sveta could swim just fine, but with danger lurking around here, she'd have to stay close.

I turned back to the car to help unload, but Mom patted my shoulder. "Go with Karey. Enjoy the muddy water and rest."

I opened my mouth to protest, but she nudged me with a hard look. I might've been the alpha female for the South Toms River pack and in my mid-twenties, but when my mother gave me marching orders, I obeyed like any good Russian girl.

A sudden movement caught my eye—a flash of silver-gray darting across the corner of my vision. I froze, my breath catching in my throat. Relief washed over me as I recognized the familiar rumble of an approaching caravan of cars. Thorn's SUV, Uncle Boris's van, and my dad's sedan appeared.

After Thorn parked the SUV and the attached U-Haul trailer beside our cars, he got out. It didn't take long for me to run up to him. He enveloped me in a warm embrace, and I briefly forgot about this damn mess.

"Did your grandma give you any trouble?" he joked.

"Oh, she wasn't a backseat driver. Mom's the troublemaker."

As the sun edged toward its zenith, our shadows withered away, leaving me and him surrounded by laughter and the buoyant Russian conversations in the air. I could sigh—for now.

"You were walking somewhere when I pulled up. Where were you headed?" he asked.

"I was checking out our scenic view."

"The pond in the picture had a lot less..." His face scrunched up.

"Algae and murky waters?" I finished for him.

We walked over to the pond where Karey chased Sveta along the edge.

Thorn let me go. "I'm gonna help the others unload. You good, babe?"

"As good as I can be."

He gestured toward the questionable chairs. "Have a seat and rest."

I shook my head and joined Karey. Those chairs were probably growing a sentient, flesh-eating bacterium.

Even if the seats needed to be cleaned, the place wasn't too shabby. A rather pleasant breeze brushed against my face as Sveta scurried my way.

"Careful!" Karey spotted her trajectory and ran to intercede. "Her hands are filthy."

"I don't mind." I picked up my niece, dirty hands and all. Every intrusive thought from my obsessive-compulsive disorder flared. Bright. Almost blinding in its intensity. All my coping mechanisms tried to kick in.

*I am safe,* I reminded myself.

Nothing on that precious child could hurt me. Sveta's sweet laughter broke through. She pointed to the chairs, and I smiled. A silver-gray titmouse landed on the top of an armrest, the bird's tiny frame trembling ever so slightly. The titmouse bolted away. Its sudden flight sent a ripple of tension through me.

"Why can't it be that easy to run away?" I whispered.

Sveta snuggled against me. I grabbed a hold of the solace she offered and didn't let go.

# CHAPTER THREE

Somehow, over ten people fit into the first cabin's living room. Between Uncle Boris and Aunt Vera's arguments and my brother complaining about the miniscule TV, I didn't have time to think about the dangers I faced. Even my cousins' empty stares from their spots in a corner made everything feel strangely normal. For the past couple of hours, the Stravinsky clan had made themselves at home. Dad had rigged the ancient television with an old VCR to play tapes for Grandma, and Uncle Boris had stuffed any random chairs into the room. Grandma was tucked away on a rocking chair while Thorn and I sat on reclining chairs. Not far from Grandma, Karey sat cross-legged on the floor with Sveta. My niece gnawed on a well-loved stuffed lion. My mom kept sewing it back together Frankenstein-style.

Home sweet away from home.

The kitchen was just as noisy as the living room. The minute we got here, Mom had commandeered the space and roped poor Aunt Olga into helping her. Every single counter was crammed with goods and now she concocted grand plans for snacks. We'd already eaten a roasted turkey dinner from a firepit. Mind you, this place didn't have one. Mom got one through manual labor.

"You look worried again," she'd said as she'd passed me a shovel. "Hard work makes people forget about their problems."

Yeah, right. Thorn, Alex, Dad, my cousins, and I dug for thirty minutes, all while my mother lorded over us.

"I want something deeper. Deeper," she'd commanded. "It should be big enough for a full buck! If not a deer, then the grave for our *enemies*!"

That got a rousing roar from inside the house.

Hours later, after we'd eaten Mom's turkey feast and Aunt Olga's potato pancakes, we grew lazy with our full bellies. I nestled in my cozy armchair with a soft flannel blanket draped across my legs. Thorn lounged beside me, his feet propped up on the wooden coffee table.

"Anna, are the chicken wings done?" Uncle Boris called out to Mom. He rested on a recliner with his feet up on an ottoman. He wore one sock and the other bare foot boasted way-too long toenails. I winced at the sight.

"You want more?" Aunt Vera rolled her eyes. "Aren't you full yet?"

"I need to keep up my strength." My uncle grinned, then popped an entire chicken wing into his mouth. His loud crunching almost drowned out the TV.

Mom left the kitchen with another batch of chicken wings. "Has anyone seen Fyodor?"

"He said something about filling up all the cars in case we had to escape," Grandma said.

Grandma's statement was simple, yet the heaviness in the word "escape" carried throughout the room. Uncle Boris's rapid chews slowed. My cousins' still faces flickered with fear. Poor Mom simply stood there, bowl in hand, as if she had nothing left to cook.

"We should make plans," Mom said with all seriousness.

"Are we going to the carnival on Monday?" Alex asked.

"That sounds like fun," Uncle Boris said. "Should draw a lot of hardy country gals."

I flashed my brother an annoyed look. "I expect us to be here for two days, tops. This isn't a family vacation."

"Lighten up, Nat." Alex grabbed a nearby pillow to get comfortable on the floor. "What would it hurt to let me take my family out for some fun?"

Thorn took my hand and stroked it. "How about we talk about that when the day comes? For now, I thought we'd decompress a bit. Maybe watch a movie or two."

Alex sighed, then called out, "I vote for *Die Hard*."

"You would," Aunt Vera replied. "I'm sick of that movie."

"Then how about *Terminator*?" he suggested.

"I'd rather not think about life-or-death chases right now," Aunt Vera admitted.

Alex replied, "True."

My uncle's relaxed expression fell away. "Fyodor is working hard to protect us. Shouldn't we tackle guard duty before we watch that movie?"

A hush fell over the room again. Uncle Boris turned off the TV, effectively shutting out the normalcy.

"We have some protections in place," Karey said. "The trees can warn me if danger is coming, but a twenty-four-hour sentry sounds like a great idea."

"I'll go first," Thorn volunteered.

"You just got off the road," I said. "Rest first. I can do it—"

We were interrupted by a sharp clap. Everyone's attention jumped to Grandma.

Her tiny form turned toward us, her dark eyes filled with reprimand. "Anna is right. We can rest in our graves. It's time to search for the great seed. Not tomorrow, but tonight."

Thorn glanced at me, and I translated her words. His head fell, then he nodded.

For a bit, no one spoke. We'd come here to find the seed, yet I was sure everyone expected more time.

"Well, then." Aunt Vera stood with a determined look on her face. She snatched the plate of wings away from her brother. "Does anyone know which way to go?"

Grandma's voice softened. "We'll learn soon enough. First, we must walk, then we'll run with Mother Moon. The sooner we begin our search, the sooner Natalya will be safe."

# CHAPTER FOUR

Not long after a decision was made, a sliver of anticipation spilled through the room. It was the full moon, after all. The thrill of the hunt added life to my weary bones. With all the issues around the Basilisk King and that damn leprechaun, I hadn't hunted with the pack during the last couple of full moons.

Karey picked up Sveta for an early bedtime while everyone else headed out. My younger brother Alex and Aunt Olga would stay behind to protect the folks at the cabin.

Once the houses were locked up for the night, we set off on foot into the cool Maine woods. The air was crisp, carrying the scent of pine and damp earth. Thorn and Uncle Boris were up ahead, leading us through the wilderness.

A part of me wished it was just Thorn and I wandering northward with no destination in mind. Back when my mate had returned to South Toms River as the prodigal son, we'd met in the woods on a night like this one. Farley had rejected my request to join the pack again, so I escaped to the woods and Thorn found me.

With just a couple of words, he'd set me off-kilter.

*"So tightly—wound,"* he'd said.

A gust of wind circled the trees and brushed against my face. The memories of that night were still vivid. I couldn't forget the way he nipped at my body and nuzzled against me. Commanded me to lose my clothes and run as a wolf with him. I obliged him, as one should.

Now, instead of hot summer lovin', we had Uncle Boris strutting up the path while Mom and Aunt Vera gabbed about the horrible prices at the local ShopRite back home. There went the nighttime ambience. At least Dad and Thorn remained stony and silent.

We walked at least half a mile before we entered a clearing in the woods. Grandma paused and bent down to touch the earth.

"Natalya," she said in a hushed tone. "Come here."

"Is something wrong?"

"We need to know where to go, so I'm going to teach you some old magic to find the seller."

A moment later, my mom stood next to us. "Mama, I don't like this."

Grandma flickered her fingers and Mom retreated with a frown.

Just hearing the term "old magic" still set me on edge. I'd used magic recently, but only sparingly since werewolf magic was against the Code, or the rules of ethics for werewolves. And for good reason. Every spell had the potential to do great things—and harm the wolf too. As a child, I'd heard Mom speak fervently about how she hated magic and those associated with it, like witches, wizards, and warlocks. Mom told me that werewolves couldn't cast spells and I'd believed her. Before I'd learned old magic, I couldn't make things appear out of thin air. And yet, after Thorn's curse worsened not too long ago, I had pushed aside those concerns to learn the magic necessary to save him.

I nearly lost myself in the process.

Grandma waited for me to speak. The seriousness in her features tugged me by the scruff of my neck like a pup.

"What do I need to say?" I finally murmured. This was a moment of truth, a step closer to finding the champion.

"You're afraid right now and that is good." Grandma stepped closer to me, bringing the scent of the Earl Grey tea she'd drunk before we'd left the cabins. "Over the past couple of months, I know you've cast spells with caution, and I believe you're ready to learn what I know before I'm laid to rest next to my Pyotr."

"Oh, Grandma," I chided. "Don't say things like that."

Grandma Lasovskaya scoffed. "We're still mortals," she whispered. "Centuries of living or not, this body won't last forever."

I sighed. Didn't all kids believe their grandparents would live forever? From elementary school to high school, I'd heard my classmates talk about death. How their elders disappeared before they had a chance to truly appreciate them.

Grandma spoke the words slowly at first. They held no weight until she took a deep breath and repeated them. It sounded like a sweet melody.

I listened intently, trying to mimic the syllables and intonations, but I didn't feel the magic rising within me—which meant I was missing a critical ingredient.

My good friend Nick, the white wizard, had told me, *"When you have the right tools—the right words, and you believe without a doubt, magic can happen."*

I did believe—so it had to be the twisty words forming knots on my tongue. "I don't recognize any of these words."

"That troublemaker Tamara taught you a great deal,"

Grandma replied, "but she couldn't teach you what she didn't know."

I eyed Grandma up and down. Her wry smile widened. That cheeky woman kept far too many secrets to herself. Even from Tamara who'd taught me much about old magic.

After I took a deep breath, I focused on the rhythm of Grandma's words. I repeated the incantations as closely as I could and let the strange sounds roll off my tongue. It was still far from perfect, but this time the words carried a hint of power. A peculiar sensation raced up my legs, like the wings of a tiny bird fluttering. The gentle sensation grew stronger and yanked me in a specific direction. My instincts told me to follow it.

"We need to go northeast toward the Nahmakanta Reserve," I whispered.

"Then northeast is where we shall go." She carefully sat down to take off her stockings. When I didn't move, she glanced up. "You got mud on your paws? It's time to surrender to the moon, girl."

I motioned for the others to shift. My family nodded and garments were draped on trees or slung along bushes. Once I discarded my jeans and T-shirt, I stooped to let the change envelope me. The wolf writhing under my skin rejoiced. It sang a happy chorus as my bones cracked and refolded themselves. My back popped and I cringed. A romantic would say our transformation was a beautiful thing, but if they were in my position, bent over with their feet breaking in two, they'd have happily kept their humanity card.

Once I was in my true form, the tranquil Maine forest shot through me with stark clarity. I held still, savoring the rhythmic hoots of the owls to the foxes observing us from their dens. There was nothing like it—which was likely why my OCD quieted in the woods. Out here, I didn't have to worry about organization. I lived only through my impulses and carnal cravings.

My family circled around me, their noses to the ground and air. Aunt Vera and Mom sniffed around Grandma's silvery form, eager to keep her close. Thorn darted away to assess for danger and returned soon after. Once I spied everyone, I bolted off to the northeast. Dad yipped from the rear, an urgent call for us to run faster. As we moved toward the enchanting pull, a new scent wafted through the air like burnt cinnamon. Thorn caught up with me to slow my pace. That smell might mean a spellcaster had been by recently, but I had an inkling the smell was connected to our destination.

As the night wore on, the terrain grew hilly, and the woods thickened. The unfamiliar territory nipped at me to turn back, but the tug grew stronger. We were getting closer. Then the woods parted to reveal the lower-lying groves to the south. We'd finally made it to Nahmakanta Reserve.

It was breathtaking.

Better than any brochure or cheesy Internet ad.

My family darted in and out of the brush, their noses to the ground, inhaling deeply. Their senses were alert, each sniff and sound vital.

Uncle Boris's ears twitched and swiveled, his eyes scanning the surroundings. Thorn darted to each of us, sniffing our flanks as he searched for Grandma.

I paused too and counted everyone nearby. We were short one.

Thorn circled the glen before returning my way. He would've yipped if he'd caught her scent. Not good. Everyone had maintained a loose formation since we had encountered no trouble.

Mom whined and Aunt Vera licked my snout in distress. Briefly, I considered doubling back—even Thorn had trotted away to search for a scent. Our tracks were still fresh. I darted back the way we came until I caught Grandma's scent. She'd followed us for a half a mile and then her tracks simply *vanished.*

A chill ran down my spine and my fear peppered the air. For someone over a hundred years old, Grandma wasn't foolish. Was something stalking us? I sniffed around Grandma's footprints, then the surrounding brush. Only a herd of deer had been by recently.

Panic fluttered through the pack. I had to do something. Closing my eyes momentarily, I tapped into the old magic again, seeking her out. As I let the magic sweep outward, a sharp tremor ran through my hind leg, making me stumble. The nip was a warning—I'd withdrawn too much energy from myself. The other wolves, sensing my distress, gathered around and nuzzled me. With a deep breath and a renewed determination, I tried again. This time, I caught a blip to the east. She was moving fast.

Had the hellhound found me already? Was it a trap?

Trap be damned, I bolted away from my family and the others gave chase.

I raced through the woods, darting around obstacles until the forest eventually gave way to a ridge overlooking a river. I came to a hard stop when I spotted a lone, two-story paddleboat sitting along the bank. Thin lines of smoke rose from a double chimney. Lanterns scattered along the second-story iron railing cast an eerie, burnt-orange glow along the black-painted ship.

A familiar pumpkin-like scent crossed my nose as we drew closer. But it wasn't the barge itself that caught my attention—it was the two figures not far from it. One was unmistakably Grandma, her distinctive silver fur making her stand out even from a distance. And I'd never forget the wisps of the night demon's chartreuse hair or the peculiar sway of her colorful skirts and peplum tops. My former employer stood no taller than my shoulder, but the way she confidently stood next to grandma sent a shiver down my spine. Tonight, Mademoiselle Midnight wore a long, black peplum top and a midnight blue leather skirt and bare feet. The wind off the river tugged at the tail of her top, but I couldn't see the end, only that it disappeared like the smoke off the chimney.

Good God, what was the demon doing here? Brenna had told me to be careful. The earth witch had been taught from a young age to avoid demons since many of them were unpredictable. I wished I'd brought my goblin blade. My time working at her rare antiques store for night spirits had ended, but I still had unfinished business. More importantly, why did Grandma leave us behind to confront the demon?

Dread seeped into me. I'd hoped for more time.

Grandma turned her head in our direction. A low growl circled from her throat. A warning.

The madame shifted her weight from one foot to the other as I shifted back to human form. Our gazes connected and she gave me a curt nod.

"I didn't expect to see you this far north, Natalya." Her green eyebrows rose in amusement. "A rather nice surprise."

"Why did you come here?" I whispered to Grandma. Not a single muscle so much as twitched on the elderly wolf's body. Her stony gaze was hooked on the demon.

I stepped between the night demon and grandma then added, "It's a surprise for both of us."

Thorn raced up to us. He bared his teeth at the night demon, but I touched the top of his head to calm him.

"Why is everyone so riled up?" the madame asked with a smirk. "I thought you and I were on better terms, Natalya."

The night demon had threatened to eat me a couple times

and I'd seen her natural form—her fifty-foot, armor-wearing, blade-brandishing get-up. Only a fool would trust her.

"Memories can be fickle," was all I managed to say.

"So they can be." She gestured toward the boat. "Since I've had the pleasure of meeting your grandmother, I should invite you on board for refreshments. Shall we?"

I gave a nod, so we made our way through the Main Deck until we reached a familiar upward staircase to the Hurricane Deck. It hadn't been that long—seemingly a little over a month since I'd been here, but the place felt different. Far quieter with less traffic from customers.

My family followed her up two sets of stairs to the final floor. At the top, the doorway to the night demon's quarters opened and revealed her private domain. The inner chamber was well-lit with endless, quivering lanterns hanging from the vaulted ceiling. I scanned the room, recognizing the sitting area to the right, her sleeping quarters in the center, and her collection of night things to the left. She coveted and collected pots and large containers of nightshade, ferns, and night-blooming moonflowers. Pretty much most of them were poisonous.

The last time I'd been in this room, we'd formed plans to confront her sister, the Daylight Dame. The daylight demon had stolen her sister's whistle and had pinned the deed on the South Toms River Pack. It took my spellcasting friends and the entire pack to fight the daylight demon's frost giant. In the process of trying to get the whistle, I had swallowed jade beads belonging to the night demon. Sooner or later, she'd wanted to collect on what she'd lost.

I strode over a glass floor in the center of the room. As I'd remembered, the strange dark waters churned underneath the thick glass. As to how this room had water below from the third floor, I wasn't gonna ask. The night demon gestured for Grandma and me to sit on wooden chairs covered in sheep's wool.

"Make yourselves comfortable," the madame said.

One of her servants, a humanoid creature with circular white coral for eyes and waist-length ferns for hair, offered us robes and cups of water. Thorn declined the water and remained near the door, his hard gaze never leaving the night demon.

My aunt and uncle—the far more curious ones—snooped around, touching plants and the various artifacts in the room. A smiling Uncle Boris idled up to one of the night servants, but my quick-handed father redirected him away.

"I don't think they want what you're *selling*," Dad hissed.

Mom approached Grandma before everyone settled in. "Are you going to tell us why you came here?" she asked her.

"I could sense her as we ran," Grandma replied crisply. "There was no better time."

"I'm surprised you wanted to speak to me on her behalf," the demon said to Grandma in crispy Russian.

"She is a good girl, but like you said earlier, she hasn't settled all her affairs with you, no?" Grandma Lasovskaya replied.

The demon's eyes darted my way. "Not completely."

"There's a little matter of some jade beads I ate," I whispered.

"You ate what?" Grandma's eyes narrowed.

"In order to pick up the Cerberus's Dog Whistle in the Daylight Dame's office, I had to eat some fire-resistant beads. It's a long story."

Grandma shook her head with disgust. "What kind of fool just picks up and eats something you don't understand—"

"At the moment I was a little pressed for time and—"

"You should know better," Grandma snapped. "Why don't you jump into a fiery pit and see if you burn?"

"Oh, *Grandma*." I sighed.

"Maybe you should find the nearest bridge, as the Americans say, and just jump off it with your little friends."

The demon sipped her spiced punch with a grin. I hoped she enjoyed my verbal admonishment. Two minutes later—with no lesson learned on my part—Grandma finished her speech and she turned to the demon.

"There is nothing that can be done about the jade." Grandma's voice lowered briefly as she added, "For now."

She addressed the demon when she said, "What matters is your compensation and when you expect to get it."

The night demon put down her cup and one of her servants scurried over to add more of the ginger and persimmon-laden drink. "You're a wise one, Svetlana Lasovskaya. I like you." She smiled. "Those jade beads had value and I expected to sell them."

"Yes, yes," Grandma said with a curt nod. "As you should."

"How much does the demon want?" Dad asked.

Mom gave him a dark look. She'd sized up the expensive furniture and museum-quality pieces the moment we boarded.

"You see, my granddaughter has fallen into other troubles," Grandma explained smoothly. "Now is not a good time —a creature of immeasurable power has sent her underlings after her."

"Diana," was all the demon said, not a sliver of emotion on her pert features.

"Yes, my night friend. Rest assured, the Stravinskys pay their debts, but we must deal with Diana and her hellhounds first."

"There is no dealing with those dogs," she said as if she'd

seen them firsthand. "You either run or you call them off with the magical tools like the dog whistle."

Back when I'd worked for the night demon, a spring fairy had stolen Cerberus's Dog Whistle from Mademoiselle Midnight's store. The whistle could summon a three-headed dog to drive the hellhounds away. I'd even gotten it back again, and yet I didn't use it for myself. The night demon had threatened to eat me, so I'd done everything in my power to return it.

I glanced toward the blackened waters beneath the glass floor. Shadows shifted below as if mysterious leviathans dipped and rose out of view.

"I've faced many foes. The divine ones are the most dangerous." She spat on her hand and extended it toward Grandma. "I will wait until Natalya is *dead* or she has dealt with the goddess. If she dies, then whoever's alive in this room can settle this debt. No?"

Dad stiffened, anger pulsing through him. Mom grasped his arm and frowned.

"What's going on?" Thorn asked, unable to keep up with the rapid Russian.

I stepped forward to handle the matter. Before anyone— namely me—could end this madness, Grandma licked her palm and shook the demon's hand.

"Grandma, you can't—" I said.

"Hush child," Grandma Lasovskaya hissed. The bite in her tone pushed me back.

I opened my mouth again, but Dad shook his head. What was done was done.

"You sound so assured I won't survive," I said to the demon. "Have you met Diana before?"

"I've met many lifeforms," the demon replied. "Some of them malevolent, some of them kind. That creature is pure *whim.* Whatever she desires—whether that is the joy of the hunt or the pleasures of mankind—she'll get."

"I don't plan to die anytime soon so I'd appreciate more time," I said bitterly.

"Thanks to your grandmother, I can give you more time." Starlight flared in her hair. "I look forward to negotiating with you again."

I sure as hell didn't look forward to it.

"Then we are good," Grandma said proudly. "One thing, though. Can you confirm there's a special store east of here?"

"Is there something you're in the market for?" the demon replied.

The two chatted as if they hadn't bargained for my life a minute ago. Dad still fumed off to the side while Aunt Vera explained everything to Thorn. Mom simply stared daggers at the demon.

"I mean a store that sells seeds…special seeds," Grandma said.

"Ah, you're seeking a store called *The Gray Glen.*" The night demon folded her arms. "My products are much better than that dryad's. Are you sure you want to find her?"

"They have what I need," I added. "I don't have a choice at this point."

"I see." The night demon's gaze settled on the wall to the west. I imagined the madame could see through it to the forest beyond. "I can confirm it's out there. Go east into the reserve. Find three hills with a set of nine pines forming a circle. What you seek is there."

"Thank you." As much as I didn't want to say it, I added, "You didn't have to help me, and I appreciate it."

"You've got enough on your plate. With the fairy murders happening around here, this area is volatile as it is."

"You know about the deaths?" I asked.

"My customers from the Old Lands don't want to come

to this area—even with all the discounts." She released a long sigh. "I tried to set a trap for the perpetrators, but so far they've eluded my night guards."

Grandma eased her way out of the seat, suddenly in a hurry to depart. "Your hospitality is beyond measure," she said sweetly. "But, no offense, we must go find *The Gray Glen*. I hope my granddaughter never needs to cross paths with you again."

The night demon took a slow sip of the red fluid, her eyes trained on our every move. "Too bad we both know it's too late for that."

# CHAPTER FIVE

After our little chat with the night demon, we escaped into the forest and headed east in wolf form. The moon hung low in the night sky, casting an eerie glow over the Nahmakanta Reserve. Tall pine trees loomed overhead, their shadows stretching out like dark fingers. The wind whispered through the branches, carrying with it the scent of pine and damp earth.

Uncle Boris and Dad kept up the hard pace behind me, while Thorn held up the rear with Grandma, Mom, and Aunt Vera.

As we moved deeper into the reserve, the mystical tug grew stronger. We were almost there. Anticipation set me on edge until I spotted something to the northeast. A circle of nine tall pine trees, their branches swaying gently in the wind. In the center stood a narrow, three-story home, as wide as a redwood tree, with bark instead of siding and a roof made of leaves and branches.

In the front yard, a simple clothesline was strung between two sturdy branches. A few garments, made of organic materials and dyed with earthy tones, danced gently in the night's breeze. Right next to the clothesline was a barrel for collecting rainwater and a tiny stone garden.

Many of the stones in the garden were painted in shades of white and gray, and upon closer inspection, tiny black dots adorned them. I found myself drawn to these dots. They seemed to pulse and move if stared at for too long, making my vision waver and my head spin slightly. I looked elsewhere—even I knew when to mind my own business.

Beyond the stone garden, a plot of rich, dark soil stretched out. This was no ordinary garden. Exotic flowers with petals streaked in vibrant shades of purple and red stood tall, their colors contrasting starkly against the night. Their sweet, intoxicating scent wafted through the air, drawing us. Interspersed among these exotic blooms were young stalks of corn and other vegetables, their green leaves rustling softly as the wind tugged at them.

As we approached, a curious phenomenon occurred. The petals of the purple and red flowers began to curl inward, closing up like disturbed clamshells. It was as if they were shy beings, retreating from the gaze of strangers. The sight was both enchanting and eerie, adding to the mystical aura of the dryad's dwelling.

Thank goodness, we'd found it.

We circled the hills twice to search for danger. Not finding any, we approached the first hill. Right outside, Grandma and I shifted back into our human forms.

The shadows hid my *babushka's* naked body, but I spotted the subtle jerk of her chin to the clothesline. "Bring me something pretty," she said.

Grandma turned to the others. "Stay here," she said. "Natalya and I will go inside."

I nodded, taking a deep breath as I approached the house. The door opened with a soft creak. It looked like a farming supply store—shelves lined with jars of seeds, tools hanging from the walls, and the scent of fresh soil and dried herbs filling the air.

A dryad stood in the center, her black hair cascading down her back and her light eyes regarding us with curiosity. She wore a simple floor-length dress made of gray cotton, and her feet were bare.

"Good day to you," I said softly. "Is this *The Gray Glen*?" I said, my voice shaking slightly. "Hope you don't mind about the clothes."

The dryad gave us a gentle smile. "Do not worry, Wolf. I am Hyacinth," she replied. "And I know why you're here."

I licked my lips and tried to calm my racing heart. Maybe we could go home soon. "If you know why I'm here, then you know I need a champion to face Diana's hellhounds."

I added, "Is it available?"

Hyacinth tilted her head, considering. "You can have it for ten bars of gold," she replied not blinking once.

"One gram each?" I squeaked.

"One pound each." Damn, she said that with her whole chest, too.

I swallowed hard. At around thirty thousand dollars apiece, there was no way I could afford it. After paying for the cabins and this trip, I barely had a hundred bucks in the bank. "I don't have that."

Grandma stepped forward. "Is there anything else we can offer? A barter worth your time?"

Hyacinth pondered Grandma's request as she picked up a rag to dust around tiny seed jars. "There's a killer on the loose," she said slowly. "They're harming my brethren from the Old Lands. I cannot leave these hills, but if you can find the culprit and restore order, you'll be more than worthy of the Seed of the Fates."

"The Seed of the Fates," I repeated. "How are the Fates related to a seed capable of summoning a champion?" My good friend Abby the Muse had spoken briefly about the three ancient sisters and how they protected her.

Hyacinth gave us a knowing smile. "How much do you know about them?"

"Not much," I admitted.

She nodded. "The Fates are powerful beings. I believe they rival the gods, but others wouldn't agree. Like Hera and her jealous ilk." The dryad snorted and Grandma nodded sagely. "There are three of them and each play a role in our lives: the spinner, the measurer, and the snipper. In your case, a divine being is trying to interfere with the length of your mortal life. The Fates hate such things. They favor the brave. If you're willing to sacrifice your life for others while yours is in peril, you will be a worthy recipient."

Briefly, I considered walking away. I had no time to hunt for a murderer. I'd likely die trying to find them. But then again, what *choice* did I have? I swallowed past the lump forming in my throat. Many bargains would be made tonight. I didn't like any of them. "I'll accept your terms. We'll find the culprit."

Hyacinth's eyes darkened. "Thank you, Wolf. You have one week," she said. "After that, *The Gray Glen* will move to Yakutia in Siberia."

"I understand." I didn't have plans to visit one of the coldest cities in the world to get what I needed so I'd have to hurry.

With a final nod, Grandma and I left the house, the door closing behind us with a soft click.

# CHAPTER SIX

The next morning arrived with a hellish nightmare. As I jolted awake, momentarily disoriented, I couldn't help but recall the weight of Diana's collar squeezing tight around my neck.

I touched my collarbone, finding nothing there. At least I was safe in bed. The quilt I had kicked off in the night was now tangled around my legs. Pulling it back up, I lay next to Thorn and tried to stop the world from spinning too fast. Too much had happened too quickly. I glanced around. Our temporary bedroom was smaller than I remembered. Wooden walls encased us, and I realized we weren't in our own bed. Instead, we were in a quaint, rustic cabin bedroom. We were in Maine.

Thorn stirred next to me, then he turned around, our noses almost touching. His hazel eyes, usually so fierce, now held a softness. He didn't speak. Instead, he gently stroked the back of my head. Every touch offered relief.

"Bad dream?" he murmured.

"That and a lot more. I had a *rough* day yesterday," I joked.

He chuckled. "Yeah, that was definitely wild."

"A little too wild for my taste."

He grinned. "Care for a bit of sunshine?"

"These walls are paper-thin. We can't do the horizontal mambo with—"

He rolled his eyes and got up. "Not *that* kind of sunshine." He fumbled through his nearby gym bag and retrieved a sealed bag. Inside of it was my beautiful nutcracker.

"I thought we'd left these with Farley…" I squealed with delight. I'd been far too busy, let alone stressed, to think about my holiday hoard. My collection had gotten me through some rough times, but the road was no place for over four hundred Christmas, Hanukkah, and even Kwanzaa holiday decorations. With my luck, a hellhound would hit the U-Haul and holiday cheer would end up strewn across the countryside.

So I'd left them behind.

I almost opened the clear plastic package, then I remembered my manners. After wiping off my hands with a sanitary wipe, I freed my friend. The wooden figure, with his hand-sewn clothes and hat, always gave me such happiness. Each time I held him, I imagined he winked at me with those little black dots for eyes. I drew him close and sucked in the scents of perfect holiday dinners and presents under the tree. Such a fantasy was best suited for children, but as a former pack pariah, I'd held tightly to the fantasy that I'd be reunited with my family again and they'd accept me, flaws and all.

"You're still handsome," I told the nutcracker.

Thorn laughed softly from the other side of the bed.

"Not as handsome as my mate, but you're close," I added.

The familiar scent of piroshkis and sausages wafted in, pulling me away from the moment.

"Let's get something to eat." I put away the nutcracker, then threw on some pants. Thorn and I trudged out of the room. Suitcases and boxes of groceries lined the hallway.

Sounds from a 1990s Russian war drama drifted down the hall from the living room. We headed to the kitchen where Mom was busy flipping something on the stove.

"Hey, Mom." I stole a still warm piroshki. Thorn had a much bigger appetite, so he grabbed a plate.

"Morning. Could you run into town and grab some more flour?" Mom asked without turning.

"You didn't buy some when we were at the store?" I took a bite and savored the seasoned ground hamburger meat and veggies covered in dough fried to perfection.

"I brought some from home, but I ran out of it after I made some cookies for the children."

That must've been *a lot* of cookies.

Mom didn't miss a beat as she flipped another pancake. "I need enough flour for the next couple of days. Grab everything they got. Check that gas station too."

I glanced at Thorn who winked at me as he stuffed a pancake-wrapped sausage into his mouth.

"Everything, huh?" I eyed the big metal bowl of pancake dough and the flour bag carcass. At least getting some flour would be a lot easier than finding a killer.

"I'm gonna knock this out before I get comfortable." I slipped on my sneakers.

"Not alone, you're not." Uncle Boris walked in through the backdoor. "Something smells good, Anna."

"I'm going with her," Thorn replied to him. "Don't worry."

"Then I'll join you two," my uncle said. "I forgot to pack a couple things."

Ten minutes later, Thorn, Uncle Boris, and I rode into town. The sun was still low, casting long shadows on the country roads. We pulled into Stitchings, not seeing too many souls visiting the shops along the main street.

"I need some coffee," Thorn said. "Anybody mind if we make a pit stop?"

The tiny coffee shop was literally across the street from the grocery store.

I shrugged. Maybe I could ask the locals—if they were supernatural—if they had any details on the murders around here. Thorn parked and we strode inside. The bell above the door announced our arrival. The place only had a single table, but the shop had plenty of old-school charm with vintage black and white photos of sailboats on the walls. The nicks and knacks sprinkled on the worn counters. Not a single speck of dirt or stains marred the surface.

Just my kind of place.

The human barista, a young man with a scruffy blond beard, waved our way without glancing up. He continued cleaning a cup, humming to himself. There went asking him questions about the murders in the area. Telling humans about the supernatural world was a no-no.

While Uncle Boris checked out the pastries in the refrigerated display, Thorn put in an order.

"Coffee, please. Add three shots of espresso." Thorn usually preferred his coffee black so we must be in for a long day.

Uncle Boris added, "Can you toss a couple of those apple turnovers in a to-go box? Some of those nutty buns too. Mama Lasovaskaya will love those."

"Not a problem." The guy's smile was unnaturally wide. The kind of cheerful that bordered on manic. "You got the last of 'em. A fella grabbed a bunch to help his daughter move to Canada. Poor thing had an arson fire last month."

Smelling an opportunity, I slid in to add, "That's a shame. Say, how safe is it around here?"

"Lady, this is Stitchings. It's too quiet. Other than that fire, nothing 'unusual' happens."

I nodded. Looks like the supernatural population kept things quiet in town.

After paying, we headed across the street to the grocery store. A pleasant summer breeze blew off nearby Moosehead Lake as tourists buzzed around the marina. A laughing couple boarded a pontoon, likely heading out for an exciting boating trip with their children.

The grocery store was eerily quiet. The radio, which yesterday played old country tunes, was silent. The aisles were empty, and the single freezer hummed softly. I peered around the store, noticing the back-office door was closed.

"Uncle, can you get the flour?" I asked. "I think I'm gonna grab some more candy for Sveta," I said to Thorn.

"You're the best aunt ever." My mate snorted. "Grab me one of those Snickers, will you?"

I nodded, heading to the counter. There, I noticed some money carelessly left behind. The tart, yet sugary scent from Patty lingered here, but something was off. The goblin blade strapped to my ankle was disturbingly silent.

"Thorn, something's not right," I murmured.

Without waiting for his reply, I moved toward the back door leading to the office. Knocking softly and hearing no reply, I tried the handle. The door opened only a crack, blocked by something. Pushing harder, I squeezed into the dark, windowless room.

A chill ran down my spine. On the floor lay the fairy clerk, her eyes still open in shock. Blood stained the wooden floorboards. I kneeled and peered at her injuries. Something big enough to fit in this space had raked its claws from her collarbone down to her belly button.

A scent lingered here—close to the floor and circling the fairy's form. Fear pulsed through me, for I'd smelled this scent before, but not recently. A werewolf had killed this woman and I'd met this person, or their pack before. Not good.

"You looking for more candy bars?" The humor in Uncle

Boris's voice died at the sight of the clerk. "Why didn't we smell her?"

"Some dead fairies don't smell," I explained, "and this is her domain."

"How did she die?" Uncle Boris asked. "Do we call the police?"

"The human police?" I glanced up at him with a frown.

"We have to do something. We can't leave her like this."

"I say we check the stores until we run into another fairy. She said her kin lived around here." I swallowed past the lump in my throat. That poor woman had warned us just over a day ago.

"I'll go lock up," Thorn offered.

"Thanks." I spied a shawl draped over the chair next to the desk. I gently laid it over her. "We need to search this place. Check for any scents or footprints."

"It's not gonna be easy," Uncle Boris replied. "A bunch of locals or tourists could come in here."

"True, but I don't believe the humans are involved. Patty warned us about this. Our killer is a werewolf."

# CHAPTER SEVEN

I discovered the phone number for Patty's husband on a cellphone bill in the tiny office. It hurt to see that Patty's family had been the carrier's customer for over a decade now. The couple had likely carved out a life here even though their children were grown and had settled elsewhere.

After calling Patty's husband, Owen, and letting my family know what happened, we waited in the store. It grew far too quiet in there with only the hum of the freezers and the roar of boats filtering through the walls from the marina. Life carried on.

We didn't have to wait long for Patty's husband to show up. A delivery van arrived quickly. I glanced out the window to see a middle-aged fellow with light brown skin and short, curly black hair. He hurried out of the car, yet paused before he walked inside. His jaw set and I couldn't imagine the emotions rolling through him.

Once he came inside, he immediately went to his wife. We went outside to give him privacy. Ten minutes later, he emerged.

"Thanks for the call, Natalya," he said to me.

"It's the least I can do." I introduced him to my mate and uncle, then I told him how we'd found her.

"I'd hoped whoever was behind those fae murders had moved on." Owen rubbed the dark stubble on his chin. "Patty was excited about having a new family settle in for a spell. Said it would be nice since the fairy folk didn't trust the shifters around here."

His last couple of words must've broken him. Poor Owen shuddered a bit, then he turned to wipe away tears.

"Is there anything else you need help with?" I asked softly. "We're gonna find who did this." I explained how a dryad had hired me to find the culprit. Owen's face fell further. It was too little too late for his family.

"There are cameras outside the marina," I added. "Any chance the marina manager will help us?"

Owen sucked in a breath and rubbed his face. He'd aged in minutes. "They're fae like us. Tell Gerhard I sent you."

Minutes later, I stepped out of the grocery store while Thorn had parting words with Owen. Instead of walking to the SUV, I stood off to the side to clear my head. My breath quickened. I couldn't shake the sight of seeing Patty like that. Too much was happening too fast.

My uncle left the store next and walked up to me. He gripped my shoulder and squeezed. "You're standing in the sun. Come sit in the car."

"Not yet." As I looked around, the world seemed oddly still. No children laughing, no dogs barking. It was as if the world knew someone had passed.

Finally, Thorn walked out and joined us. "This is bad," he breathed.

"Very bad," I echoed.

"Notice anything suspicious around Patty?" he asked.

"There weren't too many clues," I replied. "But the smell, Thorn. That smell was *familiar*."

Uncle Boris stared at the store's entrance. "But from who? Do you remember?"

I shook my head, my eyes searching the parking lot. "I usually do—I just can't pin a face to the scent. It's…from someone, but I can't put two and two together right now."

Thorn drew me into his arms. "You've been through a lot, babe. You'll remember eventually."

"I will," I whispered as my gaze flicked to the street. Cars had been in and out of the lot since the murder and their tires erased any potential tracks, but the scents remained.

"I'll get in the car in a bit," I told them. "I need to check out something."

"Then we're coming with you," Thorn said firmly.

We formed a quick plan. First things first, we needed to circle the store and see if the culprit's scent led anywhere. A quick check revealed little. I couldn't make out too many tracks in the grass, but the musky scent grew stronger as I neared the rear of the building. "They definitely came this way."

Our path led us straight to the marina and disappeared underneath the foul odors of lake muck and fish. Add on a dash of gasoline and weaker scents died a good death.

I took in Moosehead Lake to see if there was anything peculiar. It was just another lazy weekend. Not far from us, a radio blasted Lynyrd Skynyrd. Boats bobbed gently, their masts clinking softly against each other. Gulls circled overhead, their white forms darting in and out of the water.

We headed inside. The nearby marina office was a quaint, slightly dilapidated structure, with wooden panels that had seen better days. The wind chimes at the entrance jingled as we walked into a cozy waiting area. There were a couple of mismatched sofas and a coffee table strewn with boating magazines. On the opposite wall stood vending machines offering a curious mix of snacks—everything from beef jerky to gummy worms to some kind of fish bait. Eww. It was right next to the food. They could've kept the bait machine *outside*.

One corner of the room was dedicated to merchandise. Shelves were packed with mugs, hats, and T-shirts, all emblazoned with the slogan: "Find Magic in Maine: Go Boating."

The marina manager Owen had mentioned gave us a nod from the customer counter to our right. The kobold wore a glamour, hiding his greenish-gray scales and sharp eyes behind magic. He looked up from the desk behind the counter. His expression changed from indifferent to concerned when he read my pained expression.

"Need some help, ma'am?" He stood a bit.

"Are you Gerhard?" I asked him.

He nodded.

"Something's happened at the grocery store," I said softly. "Patty was killed."

Gerhard's eyes widened. Without a word, he quickly pulled out his phone and sent a text message. I could only guess he was informing others about the incident.

"Does Owen know?" the manager asked after he ended the call.

"We called him and he's at the store now."

The kobold slowly nodded. "This town is falling apart, thanks to the werewolves," he grumbled.

I quickly explained how I was helping Owen find who murdered Patty. "Can I see your video footage?"

Gerhard pondered for a moment, then he picked up the phone again. The kobold tried to keep his voice low, but we caught Owen telling Gerhard he could trust us. After Gerhard hung up, he gestured to the video equipment behind the counter. "You're welcome to see what you can find. Sorry for making you wait."

"No offense taken," I said. "This mess doesn't make were-wolves look good at all."

He led me behind the counter. The video system looked ancient, with chunky buttons and a faded screen. It seemed straight out of an '80s movie, and I wondered how it was still operational.

"What time do you want to see?" he asked.

"How about we start with last night around midnight and move forward? If Patty is like most store owners I know, she'll show up early in the morning to accept deliveries and do stocking."

Gerhard fiddled with the controls and the screen flickered to life, showing the marina at night. The silvery glow of the moonlight danced on the water, and the boats swayed gently. The kobold fast-forwarded, and I watched as the timestamp sped up. Finally, he stopped, and two figures appeared on the screen. The hunched over creatures were unmistakably werewolves. Gerhard slowed the video, and we both watched intently.

The werewolves moved with purpose, heading straight for a pontoon in the third bay. They seemed familiar with the area, as if they had been there before. As they reached the pontoon, a short human woman appeared on the screen. She looked around nervously before starting the boat. The engine roared to life, and the boat began to move, taking the werewolves and the woman away from the marina and into the vastness of the lake.

I said to Gerhard, "We need to find out where they were going. Who owns that boat?"

The kobold scratched his chin thoughtfully. "That's Todd Farrow's boat. His family has got a place off Moose Rock Road. Good folk. Never had a problem with them."

I thanked him, then we headed outside to regroup. Before

we did anything, I called my dad to pass along the awful news about Patty.

"We need to find that boat," Uncle Boris said.

"And the werewolves," Thorn added. "We've yet to see any around here."

I bit my lip and considered what we'd have to do. "That's a problem. If we find them, there won't be a warm welcome."

# CHAPTER EIGHT

Not long after we got an address from Gerhard, we jumped into the SUV and headed north. The late morning sun filtered through the dense canopy of pine and elm trees as we drove along the lakeside road. Twenty minutes later, we hit the turnoff for Moose Rock Road. The single lane path led to a beige, double-wide trailer. Other than the busted-in front door, the home was quiet and seemingly undisturbed. To the west was the lake, but the boat in question was missing. No one stirred around the house from what I could see.

Thorn parked the SUV at the end of the driveway, casting a glance at the garage and nearby shed. "Looks like there was a break-in recently," he remarked as he scanned the area.

"What do we do if we find the werewolves?" Uncle Boris's jaw twitched. "Ask 'em to say sorry?"

"We should turn them over to the dryad," Thorn said.

Uncle Boris snorted. "You think that nymph will invite them over for supper? They'll tear her apart."

"Are you sure about that?" I gave him a look.

"I've dated those chicks before," my uncle said tartly.

"Don't you remember what those nymphs did to your brother? Those women are no joke."

Thorn and I glanced at each other before we busted out laughing. Before my brother had married Karey, he'd been the golden boy of the Stravinsky family. At the time, he was the epitome of a truck-driving, womanizing, hot-blooded werewolf male. Then he crossed the wrong woman, namely Karey Nottingham. Incensed that my brother had cheated on her, she got together with her nymph sisters and broke the windows on his Dodge truck and carved quite the lovely phrase on the side. The whole family spilled out of the house to witness my brother's embarrassment, and it was Grandma who read—err misread—the words: "*Eat shit, and die, you cakesucker.*"

Oh, I'd give *anything* to have video footage of that moment.

"We should get your brother one of those custom shirts for Christmas," Thorn said with a grin. "Can we get 'cake-sucker' in large print?"

I snorted. "Definitely."

Uncle Boris frowned at our exchange. I wondered if he'd run into similar trouble in the past. "Aren't we here to check out this place?" Uncle Boris scurried out of the vehicle. Thorn and I hurried after him.

"Even if the dryad can fight them," I said. "I'd rather find a safer way to deliver the murderer."

"Agreed," Thorn said. "I promise we won't just hand them over."

As we drew closer, I examined the busted-in door, wondering if someone had made a hasty entrance or a violent exit. The goblin blade twitched on my ankle. I withdrew it as it transformed into a heavy iron blade with intricate runes carved on the hilt. A threat was nearby.

"Be careful, gentlemen," I whispered.

It took some gymnastics to get inside quietly, but eventually we reached a chaotic living room. The couch was overturned and the TV stand askew. The TV buzzed with static, its screen flickering erratically. Beyond that, the kitchen was a disaster. The two-seater table lay in pieces, while broken dishes littered the counters and linoleum floor. An acrid aroma filled the air, likely from the charred contents in the oven.

"Did the werewolves subdue the humans?" I whispered. My sweaty grip on the blade faltered.

Humans lived here, but there was another scent—not of werewolves, but of something more potent, far wilder.

A shadow moved down the dark hallway. Thorn growled. A pale woman emerged into the dim light, roughly my height, wearing jeans and a black T-shirt. Her ears were delicately pointed, and her eyes held a fervent ferocity. The bowie knife in her hand glinted when she pointed it in our direction.

"You wolves come back for more fun?" the elf asked softly.

"So beautiful…" Uncle Boris murmured. "Hello."

I raised my hands and tried to appear non-threatening. "I don't know who you are, but we're not here to fight. We just want to find—"

But the elf, with surprising speed, lunged at me, her blade set for my chest. I scrambled to the left and blocked the blow.

"Stand down!" Thorn lunged at her from the right, but with a swift snap kick, she sent him sprawling through the wall connecting the living room to the bathroom.

"Hey, can we talk about this first?" Uncle Boris joined the fray, attempting to flank her. The elf sidestepped and sent my uncle crashing through the living room window.

"Oh shit!" I didn't have time to check on him. She swung at me, and our blades connected with a sharp *clink*. Her blade blurred with each additional swing, each strike barely missing my head. Damn, she was fast. Twice I managed to slice her forearms and the cuts sizzled from the iron blade. But I could only keep up for so long. She had technique versus my speed. With a deft twist, she stooped and swept my legs. I crashed to the floor—only to have that bitch raise the blade over her head and thrust it at mine. Somehow, I rolled to the right as the blade sunk into carpeted floor.

"Damn it, can we talk *first* and kill second," I growled.

My mate hurled the kitchen table at the elf, forcing the creature to retreat. He came at her again. Swinging. Growling. She took backward shuffling steps, avoiding furniture until an opportunity presented itself. Thorn threw a punch, and she dropped her blade to grab his extended arm. She rolled hard to the left, taking him with her. He rolled under her, and she tried to pin his arm into an armbar submission, but Thorn deftly twisted out of it.

She picked up the blade again. Much faster. Oh shit.

"Thorn!" I bit out.

Thorn narrowly avoided a direct hit, but the blunt end of the blade connected with his head. He staggered back.

The elf grinned and positioned herself just right so that a beam of sunlight hit her skin. A blinding light filled the room, and when it retreated, she was gone.

I rolled onto my side, my breath ragged.

Thorn groaned and clutched the side of his head. "Was that a woman or a Mack truck?"

Uncle Boris staggered into the house nursing a wicked cut on his arm. The goose egg forming on his brow didn't look any better. "Where did that beauty go?"

"Beauty? Hopefully, *far* away," I grunted. "She hits hard."

From where I lay, I caught the sounds of something moving on the other side of the trailer. "What was that?"

The rustling noise came again, a bit louder this time.

"Yeah, that came from the bedroom." Thorn helped me get up.

Uncle Boris's gruff voice shattered the uneasy silence. "If that's another elf, we're gonna need back up," he muttered. We exchanged glances, realizing that our ordeal might not be over just yet.

Following the sound, I carefully padded down the narrow hallway. The bedroom door hung ajar, revealing an over-turned bed, a shattered dresser, and a kicked-in TV. Glass crunched under my feet from the broken bedroom window. I approached the closed closet door.

"Smells like a human," Uncle Boris whispered.

I swung open the door, ready to fight, but found a tied up and gagged middle-aged brunette. The woman's eyes widened, a mix of fear and relief flickering within them.

"Let me get you out of here." My hands worked swiftly to untie the knots, and as the fabric fell away, the woman gasped for air.

Her voice trembled as she spoke. "Thank you," she whispered, her voice hoarse.

Now that I saw her up close, I recognized her from the grainy video. "Not a problem. Do you live here?" I asked. "We're searching for a woman who took two…animals away from the grocery store."

She closed her eyes as a pained expression crossed her face. "Yeah, that was me. I'm so sorry."

The woman sniffed before she added, "The werewolves showed up last night. Beat up my husband Todd, then they made me take them into town."

Loretta knew about the supernatural world. That would make these questions much easier.

"Thorn, can you get her some water?" I asked.

Thorn left to fetch it.

"What's your name?" I asked her as I helped her stand up.

The woman wobbled on unsteady feet before she said, "I'm Loretta." Her eyes darted around the room as if still expecting danger to leap out from the shadows. I offered a reassuring smile, my senses attuned to any hint of danger.

"Did you see the elf?" I asked her.

Loretta shook her head, her eyes welling with tears. "No, just those three men."

"Did you know who they were?"

She shook her head and sobbed. "I've never met them before. They hurt someone, didn't they?"

Uncle Boris drew in a deep breath.

I sighed. At least now we knew how the werewolves secured a boat. They'd kidnapped Loretta and used her to get to town. What I didn't understand was why they'd bothered to take a human. Why not just roll up on the grocery store and leave her here?

Thorn returned with some water and Loretta gulped it down.

"Let's get you out of here." I wrapped her arm around my shoulder, and we walked into the living room.

Thorn stalked over to the broken window into the backyard. "Someone else is out there. Can you hear that?"

"What is it?" I listened a bit and tried to filter out our heartbeats and the wildlife. Finally, I picked up a faint whimpering from outside. "Someone's out there."

"Maybe it's my husband." Loretta shuffled to the door.

We hurried outside to the source: the shed. The door handle was bent inward. Whoever was in there wasn't coming out anytime soon.

"Smells like a human," Thorn said.

The goblin blade had switched back to its inert form, but I wasn't taking any chances. I got ready to strike while Thorn broke off the handle to open the door. Inside, we found a beat-up, middle-aged man huddled behind a riding mower. He thrust a pitchfork in our direction.

"Stay back," the man barked.

"Todd!" Loretta called out.

I put away the goblin blade. Todd stank of fear.

"It's okay. Owen sent us," Thorn said.

Even during our conversation, the man held firm to his weapon until he spotted his wife. I didn't blame him.

"Owen s-sent y'all?" the man stammered.

Loretta ran over to her husband and the two embraced.

"Unfortunately." I explained how we ended up here after Patty was murdered.

"Not another one." Todd glanced at Loretta who started crying again. "There's been too much killing of the magical folks."

I introduced myself and my family.

Todd gave us a curt nod and helped his wife over to the trailer steps to sit. "Never thought I'd get out of there."

"Glad to see you're safe and sound," I told him. "We came here searching for those werewolves who attacked Patty, but we only found an elf in there."

Todd managed a tired nod. "Those guys showed up right before we went to bed. Came in making a fuss. They locked me up in the shed and took my wife with them."

"Do you know anything about the elf?" Uncle Boris asked.

Todd spied the broken door to his home and his voice thickened. "That would be Calliope. Not sure who hired her to come to Stitchings, but she's been chasing after those shifters for over a week now."

We followed the couple inside where Todd rushed to the sink for a drink of water. When he'd quenched his thirst, the man took in what was left of his home.

The silence grew heavy until Uncle Boris spoke. "Do you

know why all this is happening? Why are the fairies and werewolves fighting?"

Todd hesitated, then said, "It's all one big mess, if you ask me."

Loretta slowly shook her head. "A couple months ago, one of the fairies cursed a troublemaker werewolf. After that, the murders started up."

I sighed, realizing the gravity of the situation. "We need to find those werewolves or your boat. Do you know where they might've gone?"

Todd shook his head. "I heard a bunch of cars peel away after the boat left."

I asked a couple more questions, like did his boat have GPS, or if he recognized any of the werewolves, but he answered no to all of them like Loretta—which meant we had no leads as to where the werewolves went. Our elf had vanished into thin air too. We had more intel, but we were still stuck at square one.

We drove through town a bit—what little town existed—before we returned to the cabins. No one said a word. Maybe Thorn and Uncle Boris were lost in thought too. So much had happened from Patty's death to our attack at the Farrows' house. Did I need to mention a goddess's hellhound wanted to drag me down to Jersey for an eternity of hanging out with Diana?

Our bruised trio returned to quite the cookout. The Stravinskys had spilled out of the house and now they sat on the lawn chairs, kitchen chairs, and even stools around Dad's fire pit.

"Did you learn anything?" Mom turned to one of my younger cousins. "Go make three plates."

"Don't worry about it," I said. "I'm not hungry."

She took in my face. "Your father said something happened to Patty at the store."

I nodded as everyone quieted.

Dad stood from his seat. "What happened after you left the marina?"

"Oh, boy." Thorn ran his hand through his blond hair.

"A lot." I filled everyone in on poor Patty, our time at the marina office, and our attack at the Farrows' place.

"This is bad," Mom whispered.

"I don't like this, Natalya," Dad admitted. "We shouldn't get in the middle of a turf war. I know how these things end and it won't be pretty if we interfere with another pack's affairs."

"If we don't find out who killed the fairies, then we won't get the seed." Mom spoke with dead finality.

"Also, we can't stay here forever," I added.

Mom tried to smile a bit, even though I caught her distress. "Why not?" she asked. "Mama is happy here."

Grandma gave me a soft smile.

"Even if Grandma likes Maine, this isn't our home," I replied. "I also don't like forcing everyone to protect me. Even Karey looks tired."

My sister-in-law sat on a blanket next to a sleeping Sveta. Her normally light-blue eyes had dimmed, and her glistening skin appeared dull.

Alex was sitting next to his wife. "She's right. We can't keep this up indefinitely."

"Sasha—" Mom's face darkened.

"No, Mom." He shook his head when one of my cousins offered him more food. "Karey can't keep listening to the woods forever. She's using up a lot of magic."

"Is it like a phone?" Mom asked. "Why can't she just hang up?"

That got a frown from her son. "I don't know how nymph magic works, but I know it's not infinite."

"Then we'll let her rest," Dad said firmly. "Boris or myself can do patrols."

Uncle Boris took a seat. He already had a beer in hand. "Been a while since we've searched for our enemies like in the war."

"The war?" I asked.

"Your uncle fought in Germany, Korea, and Vietnam too," Aunt Olga said proudly.

"How come you never told me about your service?" I asked. He pretty much bragged about everything else.

"I'm not particularly proud of those days," Uncle Boris admitted. "Just like when your dad worked for the mafia in Atlantic City."

My dad was a powerful werewolf with a menacing build. He'd spent my childhood working as a bodyguard for the supernatural crime groups. During his time, he'd done many horrible things—including incurring a moon debt to the werewolf Russian mafia. For werewolves, a moon debt wasn't a monetary obligation, but one that can only be paid in blood or sweat. According to the Code, my father's debt had to be repaid. I fulfilled his obligation to the mafia by delivering a fairy child to the Jackson pack in Maine. Of course, things went awry during the delivery, but in the end, we returned the child to her family, and my friends and I defeated the Jackson pack.

Now I was back in Maine, and I faced werewolf problems again. I sighed. Maybe we should've driven south. We could've kept going until we reached the southern tip of South America, but even I knew the ends of the earth didn't matter to a goddess.

# CHAPTER NINE

Instead of running into Grandma in front of the TV knitting a sweater, I found her outside the house. She perched on the edge of the seat while her gaze was trained on the moon above.

"Is everything all right, Grandma?"

She gave me a sweet smile. "Just thinking of old times," she said. "After you've lived for a long time, memories start to blend together, but the powerful ones—the ones you shouldn't forget—remain fresh."

I couldn't imagine what she'd experienced—losing Grandpa, moving away from her homeland, all those things had colored her world.

"Are you remembering your time in the new world of America or Russia?"

She didn't speak for a bit, her hands resting in her lap. Briefly, I wondered if I'd brought up something painful.

"Recently, I've thought about you," she admitted, "and what you need to survive. I've wrestled with the skills I have taught others."

"You mean Tamara."

"Yes, at the time, I thought she'd take what she'd learned and use it for the betterment of all werewolves, but that woman turned it into a money-making enterprise." She shook her head with disgust and untied the scarf around her head, revealing her long, silver hair.

Usually, Aunt Olga braided it, or on the days when Grandma didn't want anyone fussing, she did it herself while she watched TV. Seeing her running her fingers through the strands brought back such memories from my childhood. I wished I could've seen her younger face—her bright brown eyes assessing me without the harder years added in.

Grandma continued. "I wanted Tamara to protect herself once she learned the more potent spells. For there were other bad people back then. They wanted to learn old magic too, but they had heinous plans in mind." She sighed. "There's another spell I want to teach you. I have only used it three times as a final resort."

I turned my back to her, not wanting to know what she meant.

She drew her fingers through the strands. "Do you remember when the Long Island Pack attacked us at your parents' house after Peter and the others had been drugged with the Chinese food?"

I remembered that night well. I was hiding from the Long Island Pack after their owner had put out a kill order for me. I'd crossed him ages ago and he'd wanted to settle the score. That night, my grandmother had revealed she knew old magic and she cast a most frightening spell. In the end, she became a horrid monster to protect me.

"I don't want to know, to be honest," I said.

"I said the same thing to the woman who taught me old magic. Some spells shouldn't be cast. Some words shouldn't be said, but my child, we must sometimes do things we don't want to do to protect ourselves or the ones we love." I could sense her gaze on my back. This time her soft-spoken voice had an edge to it. A firmness. Svetlana Ludmilla Lasovskaya meant business.

"How did you learn it?" I asked to buy myself some time to consider.

Grandma's movements stilled. She drew a deep breath. "It's a long story."

"I haven't got much else to do."

"No, you don't," she replied. "I wish I could say it was like those dramas I watch. You know, the ones where a spunky heroine slips through the door to a hidden world of magic and mystery, but it wasn't.

"It all started when I was visiting my aunt Lada for the spring." Grandma's face grew wistful. "Her first baby was coming, and Mama didn't want her to be alone. Not that my aunt needed it. Back then women birthed their babies, then they strapped the babe to their chest and worked the fields, but that's not what I should point out. It was how I'd found her. When I was crossing the fallow barley field near their house, I heard breaking glass and saw my uncle storming out. He had fire in his eyes and clenched fists. I'd never seen him like that before—he'd always been kind to my family. And yet, when I walked in, I was shocked to see Aunt Lada wiping away blood from a split lip. She'd already started to heal, but even I could see where he'd punched her."

"Your uncle beat her?" I breathed. "Why?"

"He was a bitter man. His father had abused his brothers." She gave me a long look. "It was different back then and your aunt told me to never tell anyone."

"I can imagine it was difficult—wait, how did you learn old magic?"

Grandma gave me a sly smile. "I was getting to that. Not long after I'd arrived, I happened to discover Aunt Lada practicing old magic." Grandma chuckled. "Even back then, it was forbidden, but that morning I heard her whispering words over the porridge she gave uncle. The man never complained about the taste, only about his aching joints as he worked. As February turned to April, he started to limp. By the time my aunt's sweet boy was born, my uncle was bedridden."

"She *poisoned* him?"

"I couldn't believe it either. I'd wake up in the morning, and I heard her using old magic as if it were nothing. She cooked her food without hauling firewood, mended her clothes without needles. Plowed and planted seeds in her fields. It was breathtaking to see—she just made everything look *easy*." Grandma giggled. "One day, while Aunt Lada slept-in, I got up early and decided to help. I stooped before the fire like a thief in the night and tried to cast my first spell. I'm sure you can guess how it went."

My first-time summoning fire in Tamara's kitchen came to mind and I laughed. After learning the words to cast water spells, I'd moved on to fire and blew up an old piece of toast.

Grandma continued. "I blasted a hole through the hearth and set the trees behind the house on fire."

I busted out laughing and Grandma joined me.

"Us Lasovskaya girls know how to pack a punch." I told her about my mishap with fire.

"After my aunt fixed the house while I held the baby, I expected her to punish me, but she asked me what I knew instead. She was quite surprised to learn I'd remembered everything." Grandma tapped her head and gave me a conspiratory grin. "The women in our family, minus your mother, have a knack for memorization."

"Tamara told me something similar. She said, 'Memory is a tricky game, and when it comes to knowing things that can potentially save your life, you either know it or you don't.'"

"She's right. The words are the first step." Grandma

murmured words under her breath. A breeze rustled the trees, then swept across the pond. The wind picked up strands of Grandma's hair and braided them. Once the last tendril of hair was in place, she added, "Belief is the second. Are you ready to learn more?"

"So I can make more trouble?" I asked with a laugh.

"No, but you'll be able to never become one of Diana's hunting dogs again."

I couldn't deny the stern expression on her face, so I nodded.

"Then let's begin. We'll start small." Grandma touched the back of her right hand with her left one. "I'll speak these words twice, and you will mark and remember them."

Grandma spoke seven words—far more than most of the spells I knew. When she was done, she presented the reddish fur on the back of her palm. "Now it's your turn."

I glanced at my fur-free hands as anxiety touched my senses. I could almost imagine myself standing in Tamara's kitchen again. The dark-haired, middle-aged woman had stood over the double sink and taught me fire spells.

After a quick prayer I wouldn't change my hand into a toilet plunger, I recited the spell. I let the words glide across my tongue. A tingle spread across my skin, like a fingertip circling the surface, but nothing happened. I was close. So wonderfully close. I spoke again, but this time with urgency. Finally, the telltale scent of ozone crossed my nose.

After all that work, I managed to sprout a mangy looking, single patch of red fur.

Grandma leaned closer to peer at my handiwork, but we both knew I'd messed up.

"Not bad," she murmured.

"It looks like a rabid red panda," I blurted out.

"Kind of." She whispered the words again and tapped my hand. The patch disappeared as quickly as it had appeared.

Grandma added, "It's your first time doing this spell and you even channeled the power without hurting yourself. Baby steps, my *vnuchka*. With the mistakes you've made in the past, you may not believe in yourself, my granddaughter, but I do. I always will."

# CHAPTER TEN

My life and death lessons with magic didn't begin on that fateful night I'd seen Grandma use old magic firsthand. Oh no, when you dealt with the supernatural world every day, the lessons came early. Mine arrived when I spent the afternoon at my good friend Jennifer McGuffin's house. Since both of our dads worked as machinists at a factory near town, it was easy for us to hangout and have her dad or mine drop me off before bedtime.

On that particular Friday thirteen years ago, we'd walked home from middle school together. As eighth graders, we were looking forward to high school next year and the cuter —albeit not so mature—boys.

"What are you doing this summer?" Jenn asked.

"I have to go to Camp Harold," I grumbled. Every attempt I'd made to appear *normal* like other werewolf kids had failed, so my parents had warned me about getting shipped off.

*"There's nothing you can say to change my mind. It's for the best,"* Mom had said.

Dad had added, *"Listen to your mother. You'll be* normal *in no time."*

Normal, huh?

"That sucks," Jenn said. "My cousin had to go to one of those nymph camps outside of Atlantic City. Said she hated it."

As we trudged through a back alley to Jenn's house, I considered what I'd have to do to avoid going. Dad had already made the down payment for registration and Grandma's protests hadn't worked. My quirky behaviors—from washing my hands too often to obsessing over trivial things –had gone on long enough. A couple weeks of roughing it in a tent and doing trust falls with my peers was just what the doctor ordered.

"I want to stay here and finish our project," I said firmly.

"At the rate we're going, we should have that birdhouse done before school ends."

The thing was, I didn't want to be done. Being done meant Jenn didn't have an excuse to invite me over every weekend. Perhaps I'd hoped Jenn's family would adopt me and I wouldn't have to deal with that stupid camp.

Unfortunately, as we arrived at Jenn's house, nobody jumped out and declared that I was their long-lost child.

The house was quiet since nobody was home yet. Both of her parents worked at the factory. Jenn and I abandoned our shoes in the living room. The first time I'd walked in here, I found it peculiar that the TV wasn't left on and there weren't any snacks to eat in the kitchen. Jenn's mother was a brownie, yet she kept a human's home. The place had a cozy couch set from a nearby furniture outlet, family photos stylishly arranged like the ones in magazines, and the sink never had dirty dishes in it.

"You want some fairy snacks?" Jenn asked.

"No thanks." Those things tasted amazing, but the last time I ate one, I had gas for days.

Jenn plodded up the steps and I hurried after her. The rooms up here were just as showroom worthy as the downstairs. Jenn's room smelled like someone had doused the place in fabric softener. My nose wrinkled at the scent as my gaze swept over her wrinkle-free paisley print bedspread and her organized desk. If I weren't mistaken, each pencil was arranged in a perfect fan. I snorted. My uncle Boris would say those perfectly sharpened pencil tips could be used as a shiv in an emergency.

"Do you guys have maids or something?" I couldn't help asking.

"Kinda." She gave a half-shrug. "Mom said our kin takes care of it."

"Kin?"

"We're Scottish and Grandpa brought over some brownies from the Old Lands." She shrugged as if everybody did that. "I never see them, so I don't care."

Jenn fetched our project from a shelf above the desk. Our burgundy birdhouse—now adorned with intricate, white-colored swirls—was much prettier than the yawn-inducing ones we made in shop class.

"I think we should add a strip of fairies and wolves on the lower half of the house," she suggested.

Now that would eat up *a lot* of time. "Great idea."

She ran her finger along the spot. "The fairies should have knives, and the wolves should have sharp bloody teeth."

My gaze flicked in her direction, but I said nothing. If I lived in a sunshine-high-on-life household like this one, I might've clung to morbid things too.

"I'll get the paint." Jenn handed me a bright orange plastic cup. "Can you get some water?"

"Sure."

We usually painted outside, but it was way too windy today. Jenn arranged a paint tarp on the floor while I headed to the upstairs bathroom.

Except for the hum of the air conditioner, the house was deathly silent as I headed to the bathroom. I'd never been in this room before. We usually worked outside or in the dining room. Just like Jenn's bedroom, the bathroom boasted shiny surfaces, along with pearl square tiles. I had to give it to Jenn's mom. At least, she knew the right fabric to use for hand towels.

I approached the sink and placed my hand on the faucet handle to turn it, but I noticed something strange. There was a dim light coming out of the medicine cabinet. Faint whispers filtered out from within.

*Now that's weird as hell.*

Usually, or perhaps I should say most of the time, I minded my own business. But it wasn't every day you spotted what looked like a bedside lamp shining out of the corner of a medicine cabinet. Unable to resist, I reached for the corner.

What the hell did they have living in there?

The moment my hand touched the cold metal along the edge, the bathroom lights went out. I immediately backed up as a growl circled in the back of my throat. Even the light emanating from the medicine cabinet was gone. I scrambled backward, hoping for my back to hit the door, but I just kept moving. Step after step. The whispers grew louder until I could understand them.

A high-pitched voice near my ear said, "So dirty."

Another voice, far too close to the top of my head, added, "Filthy, filthy, wolf. You don't belong here."

"Please leave me alone," I mumbled.

"We should fillet you until we see the white of your bones," a third deep voice added with a chuckle.

I shuddered.

"We'll bleed you good for soiling our home." A sharp sting raked across my shoulder blade, then another painful scratch ran down the back of my ear.

"Jenn?" No one answered me.

I turned around and bolted. My footsteps made no sound. The air conditioner's hum had long faded. No matter how hard I ran, the scratches kept coming on my forehead and on the back of my hands. The stings were short-lived at first, then grew in intensity as the tiny, invisible blades cut deeper.

When one of my attackers sliced the skin right below my left eye, I stooped to cover my head. I was probably gonna die in a bathroom. It couldn't get any worse than that.

I wasn't sure how long I protected myself, but the wolf writhing under my skin nipped at me to act. Its anger grew until its rage pulsed within me. My claws lengthened from my fingertips, and the growl growing in my chest deepened. Even if I couldn't see this enemy, I'd put up a fight. I stood again and clawed at the darkness.

Laughter erupted from everywhere. "Does the dirty wolf want to fight?"

"I'm not dirty," I replied. "Before you judge anyone, what do you have to say for yourselves? Show me what you look like first."

The chuckling cut off. "Does this rabid dog wish to see us?" the high-pitched voice said.

The second voice said, "The filthy creature will pay after we show them."

A white light flared to my left. It was so bright I had to briefly turn away until it dimmed. What I found surprised me. It wasn't three brownies but one. The grubby looking fellow stood as high as my waist and wore dark brown overalls and shiny boots. Tufts of his white hair were shorn close to his scalp. The brownie's skin was so pale, I could make out the blue veins scattered across his wrinkled cheeks.

"Can you see me now?" He spoke with a rough Scottish burr.

The back of my legs tensed up to attack, but what good would that do since I was in his domain. He had all the power here. I'd have to set myself free.

"I highly doubt I'm dirty," I said. "I want proof."

Now that had taken the brownie aback. "Well," he mumbled. "Your clothes are dirty."

"By what definition? I had gym today, but I showered afterward."

His frown deepened. "Your hands are filthy. I could tell when you picked up the cup."

I folded my arms, not wanting to go there. "My hands are clean."

"Oh, really now." His dark brown eyebrows rose in disbelief.

I opened my mouth with a saucy retort but couldn't force myself to lie. I recalled—with vivid clarity—everything that set me off today: the banister at school, the slimy basketballs during gym, and even the disgusting drinking fountains.

Finally, I presented my palms and said, "I washed my hands four times this afternoon."

He gave me, then my outstretched hands, a long look as if he finally saw me.

"At least you're cleaner than the McGuffin fledgling," he admitted.

He must've been referring to Jenn. My friend walked about without a care. If she didn't have Cheeto crumbs on her shirt or pencil smudges on her wrist, you'd suspect that she was a carefree person, but she was like everybody else. Nice and normal. Unlike me.

My minor wounds had already started to heal, but I wasn't done with the brownie.

"You better set me free. I mean it," I said firmly. "If you don't, I'll tell Jenn's mom what you did to me."

"And she'll do what?"

He had a point there. Jenn's mom tolerated this mess.

"Then I'll come back with my pack," I warned, "and we'll *mark* this house over and over again. How about some werewolf excrement to brighten up your day? My little brother sure would get a kick out of that."

The bathroom lights switched on again. I was standing in the middle of the bathroom with the filler orange cup in my hand. The tiny light underneath the medicine cabinet switched off with an audible *click*.

Instead of standing there like a fool, I frowned at my reflection in the mirror and returned to Jenn's room. Of course, my friend hadn't heard a thing. She kept humming to herself while she set up the tiny containers of paint. I ran my fingertips along my cheek to find the scratches had healed up already. The one on the back of my leg would take a lot longer, but Jenn didn't need to know that.

"Can we do this at my house?" I managed to say. The confidence I'd had when I'd confronted the brownie had leaped out the window, rolled across the lawn, and was now halfway to the river.

She glanced up at me. "Something wrong?"

Apparently, she hadn't heard me running a marathon around her bathroom. "Your kin just used me as a scratching post."

Her mouth dropped. "Are you serious? It didn't hurt you too badly, did it?"

I told her what happened. I gotta say, the look of horror on her face made me feel bad.

She packed up the painting supplies. "This is bad. It's never attacked people before."

Wow, that poor brownie didn't even have a name.

"I really should've ignored that light," I admitted, "but that's no excuse for what happened."

"No, it isn't." She sighed. "My mom's gonna pitch a fit."

"How often do you have 'people' over?" I used air quotes around the word 'people,' then I picked up my backpack. The sooner I got out of here, the better.

"We don't have humans over. Mom says they're *nasty* creatures."

"Do you really believe that?" I edged toward the doorway.

"Of course not." I caught the lie. Jenn's heartbeat picked up and she tried her darndest not to break our gazes.

"Let's go," I finally said. I left the room, briefly glancing at the closed door to the bathroom. No matter the prejudices or quirks in this house, I had to be careful from now on. Whether I was *normal* or not, I had to be brave.

Now that I lay next to Thorn to rest for the night, I couldn't help but think of that fearful afternoon and my eventual trip to Camp Harold. Even though I'd hated the changes in my routine, I'd survived—and I'd even met my best friend, Aggie. Now all I had to do was save myself from Diana. Just like my confrontation with the brownie, I wouldn't go down easily. Grandma's lessons would serve me well.

# CHAPTER ELEVEN

Even at a time when pups should still be sleeping in their beds, the cabins were loud with the Stravinskys underfoot. I slept off and on, unable to shake the sight of Patty from my head. Yesterday had been an absolute disaster. I needed to speak to Owen again, but now wasn't a good time. His spouse had died recently.

I tried to turn over and sleep again, but I caught the sounds of my mother bustling about in the kitchen. The tantalizing scent of sizzling bacon and freshly brewed coffee drew me out of bed. Thorn continued to snore and didn't stir.

I found Mom at the kitchen table reading a magazine. Uncle Boris and Grandma sat in the living room watching river fishing on the public TV channel.

"Couldn't sleep?" she asked.

"Not really," I replied. "Is Dad out on patrol?"

She glanced at her watch. "He should be back any time now."

As if on cue, Dad opened the back door and shuffled into

the kitchen. Overnight his stubble had settled in, leaving his features weary.

"Morning." He kissed the top of Mom's head.

"See anything out there?" I asked.

"Nothing you need to worry about." He rubbed the top of his balding head and sat in the seat opposite Mom, who got up to make him some coffee.

Grandma ambled into the kitchen. "Before we get too busy today, I want to stop by the grocery store to pay my respects."

"We should go another time," I replied.

The room fell silent. Only the sound of sizzling bacon filled the room.

Dad cleared his throat. "Let's finish breakfast and go as soon as possible. We can offer our condolences."

With a decision made by my elders, the Stravinskys piled up in two cars and left for the grocery store an hour later. As we approached the place, the mood in Mom's car grew somber. The brightly colored trucks, RVs, and carnival equipment rolling in from the south didn't brighten our spirits.

I swallowed back a sigh as Sveta's head jerked toward the flashy pictures of animals and clowns. She pointed at the folded-up Ferris wheel.

"Maybe later, sweetie," Karey said.

We parked in front and I couldn't miss the black and white CLOSED sign taped on the door.

We weren't the only ones paying a visit. A group of humans milled about outside. They were speaking in hushed tones to Owen.

The Stravinskys got out and approached everyone. Dad went up to Owen first and shook hands with him. Then he introduced us. Each Stravinsky paid their respects.

"God will care for her," Grandma said softly in broken English.

"It's absolutely horrible what happened," Mom said.

Owen's eyes met Mom's. "Thank you for coming. I heard from Patty about your family. I wish we could've gotten to know each other under different circumstances."

A flustered human woman stepped forward with cash in hand. "I know it's a lot to ask, Owen, but could I get some baby food? I'll be in and out real fast."

Owen stuffed his hands in his pockets. Underneath his short nod, I caught his hesitation. Who'd want to walk into the place where your wife had died? "Of course, of course."

This place was the only store for the next twenty miles. Had the pair run the place by themselves this whole time?

I stepped forward. "I can help. I'm a store manager back in Jersey. Why don't you let me handle things for a bit?"

Owen shook his head. "You don't have to. I've got it."

"Nonsense," Mom said firmly.

Even Grandma took his hand and gently patted it.

Owen glanced at each of us. Technically, we were still strangers in a way.

"If it would make you feel more comfortable, you can see my ID too," I offered.

Finally, he managed a nod and gave me the keys. "Thank you, Natalya."

Minutes later, the Stravinsky clan had the store open again. I busied myself at the register, feeling a pang of sorrow as Owen handed me some bills and change for the machine. He departed as quickly as he'd arrived.

Mom whispered to me, "Poor man. I can't imagine what he's going through."

As I rang up items for the customers, Mom and Aunt Olga bagged up everything. Aunt Vera and her children restocked the shelves.

While the others worked, Grandma crafted a simple wreath from grass and branches she'd gathered outside. She slowly made her way to the back-office door, placing the wreath gently against it. Bowing her head, she murmured a prayer for Patty. The act was simple, but it spoke volumes. The store, which moments ago had been filled with the cacophony of commerce, fell silent.

Mom whispered in Russian, "It's beautiful, Mama."

Grandma nodded, her voice filled with emotion. "Lord knows no one deserves to die like that."

The day wore on, and the Stravinskys kept the store going until the late afternoon. When it was time to close, we left the mournfully sweet scent of grass and hope behind.

After locking up the store, we left the building to a too-bright sky. The sun wouldn't be setting for another couple of hours. That didn't stop Uncle Boris and Alex from marveling at the carnival. All it took was a single workday for the business to set up shop in the nearby marina parking lot.

I'd tried to ignore it throughout the day, but who wouldn't notice a kaleidoscope of colors and sounds bustling with infectious energy outside your window.

Without casting a glance over his shoulder, Alex took Karey's hand and hefted his daughter over his shoulders. He started to walk over to the marina parking lot.

"Should we go home first so Mama can rest?" Mom suggested.

"How about I take your mother back to the cabins? We should let the young folks have some fun," Dad said. "We may not have another chance like this for a while."

The way they looked at each other, it seemed like a whole

conversation had taken place. Mom nodded and whispered something to Grandma. The older woman plodded over to Mom's minivan.

With a decision made, Dad would drive Grandma, Mom, and Aunt Olga back to the cabins while everyone else headed over. My brother was already showing his child the sights. Sveta kept pointing at the flashing lights from the Tilt-A-Whirl, while my cousins' eyes lit up. Aunt Vera reluctantly handed over some cash and they escaped into the crowd.

Thorn slipped his right hand in my left. "Should I win you something?"

"Yes, you should."

Uncle Boris scanned the mixture of humans and supernaturals covered in glamour. "I wonder if that Calliope woman will be here?"

"Probably not," Thorn said. "She didn't seem like a people person."

"She seemed more like a kill-people kind of person," I added.

"Sounds like an amazing woman," Uncle Boris said as he nodded. "She'd hunt down your food, skin it, then she'd have many tales to tell as we sipped wine long into the night."

I shook my head. It seemed like every woman would be his ideal.

We weaved through the humans, many of them screaming and laughing through their conversations. A group of human women held a quilt-a-thon at one long table while others gathered in a bustling single-tent beer garden. Glasses of beers flowed freely, and the humans eagerly parted with their cash.

We passed Alex who had stopped at a milk bottles booth game. With ease, he knocked over the stack of bottles and won a prize for Sveta.

Next, we passed my cousins who had gotten into line for

the Tilt-A-Whirl. They engaged with some other sullen-looking teenagers. I smiled and Thorn's grip on my hand tightened.

"It's good to see you relaxed and having fun," he said.

"How come you and I have never gone to an amusement park?" We'd never made the trip, yet the idea of sitting in those same seats or touching those handlebars after those humans put their grubby, nasty hands all over the place didn't seem appealing.

Thorn chuckled. "We get enough thrills from everyday life these days—not that I didn't want to take you. I'd like to travel the world with you, but we keep running into the kind of trouble where I just wanna sit in the middle of nowhere and do nothing."

The thought of doing absolutely nothing—of just sitting in a blank, sterile white room—seemed divine. Almost impossible. I'd planned a Maine trip with Thorn to tap into serenity, but as he'd said, we'd never had a moment to catch our breaths.

"How about you win me a prize over there?" I pointed to a water gun horse racing game on the other side of the lot. "Then we can sit down in the beer garden and plan out our quiet, serene, no drama vacation."

After I said those words, Thorn leaned over and kissed my forehead. The gesture was heartfelt, but when he pressed his lips against my skin, I didn't believe we could plan a vacation in the future. Maybe I couldn't see the future anymore now that I had Diana in my life.

Once we made it to the booth, the lady behind the counter said, "Looks like we have some customers. Care to play? A dollar each."

The human appeared eager to make a sale.

"No cheating," I whispered.

"How am I supposed to win?" Thorn replied just as

quietly.

"You're an excellent shot," I said. "Just try." I eyed him to show that I wouldn't allow any cheating.

Thorn lost not once, but twice, before I gave in.

"Fine," I whispered. "I want that Santa doll. You can stop playing now."

He flashed me his award-winning grin, then he won with ease. After watching Thorn get a near perfect score, the woman blinked for a moment. Finally, she handed me the prize, a cute little Santa Claus doll dressed in a red riding suit as he sat upon a reindeer in full racing horse regalia. I squealed with joy. You didn't have to be home to add to your hoarding stash.

Suddenly, someone bumped into me. Usually, I ignored it. We were in a crowd, after all. But a scent crossed my nose—one that I had smelled on Patty's body. I handed over the doll to Thorn and bolted after a man wearing a green hat with white trim. He was a werewolf. The man's scent was faint, but it blended well with the sweaty human bodies and other supernatural creatures around us. I weaved through the crowd as the man's pace picked up—only for him to disappear into the sea of faces. And he wasn't the only one wearing that hat. Another human passed and I caught the same text on the front: *Granger Cranberries*.

Thorn caught up with me. "Did you recognize someone?" he asked.

"It was the smell I caught on Patty."

Thorn searched through the crowd. "I don't smell it."

"It was faint, and there are too many people here." We walked through the carnival again, stopping at every booth. At every ride. Other than my family members, we never encountered another werewolf again.

Either the culprit had disappeared, or someone was playing with me.

# CHAPTER TWELVE

After the carnival, everyone returned to the cabins. While Dad and the others were debating on how to catch the culprit, I escaped the house to go speak to Grandma again. Instead of finding her next to the seats near the fire pit, I spotted her sitting on the other side of the pond. She perched at the edge and her bare feet dangled into the cool waters. As I drew closer, she even wiggled her toes and splashed a bit. Hearing her girlish giggle made me smile.

"Come, come," she beckoned me.

I hurried over and discarded my shoes before I sat. The water along the edge appeared gross with algae lapping against the shore.

"There's nothing in here that will hurt you," she said softly. "I want you to feel everything around you tonight so you can connect with something other than yourself."

After taking in the water, I took my time to slip off my socks. The grass tickled the sensitive skin between my toes, but it would take me a moment—a bit longer than a moment —to finally sit next to her with my feet in the water.

Once I gave in and took the plunge, she nodded with approval.

"There you go. See?" She demonstrated by lifting her feet in and out of the water. "Feels nice, no?"

"Feels amazing." The temperature had dropped as mother moon rose in the sky, but the water still retained heat from the day. If I closed my eyes and didn't look so closely, I could imagine that the water was crystal clear, and that a universe didn't live within the waters squirming between my toes.

"Today we'll go into another lesson. Yesterday, you learned about self-transformation. Now, we'll talk about transforming something *else*."

I tried not to sigh. Drawing from within to accomplish what I wanted was one thing, but to change something else rubbed my fur the wrong way.

Grandma must've caught my sullen mood, for she said, "Oh, stop it."

Then she added, "I'm not having you go out and curse people or transform them into pigs. Such a thing would be an insult to the hog, but it's important for you to learn these powerful spells and use them if needed."

I sighed. "I don't mind learning them. I'm wary since we're pretty much jumping into the deep end of the pool with this stuff. Tamara only taught me the basics for a reason."

"Oh, Natalya," Grandma said.

"Mom didn't want me to learn either."

"My Anna means well. She's right to be cautious. The zealous old magic spellcasters take what we know, and they taint it, but you're a good girl. I trust you."

She fished in her dress pocket and withdrew a large, red apple. It was so ordinary that I couldn't resist laughing.

"How did you get that out of the house without someone eating it?" I asked.

"It wasn't easy." She handed it to me and continued. "This is what you'll change."

"How?"

"During the last lesson, I wanted you to feel for something other than yourself, and you have already started to do that. When you'd opened yourself to old magic in the past couple of months, you'd opened yourself to the flow and ebb of living things. Now I want you to reach out to the inert ones like this apple."

I examined the apple, finding it firm with only a small bruise. It even still had the stem from when it'd been connected to its tree.

"I can feel it in my hand," I murmured. "And I can perceive its weight, but I can't truly *see* it, if you know what I mean. How do you feel for something with no underlying magic?" I felt foolish for asking such a question, but it seemed like an obvious one.

"Think about it. You take from yourself to cast spells and you understand how that works. Now when it comes to this inert object, you can tap into every single part of it, too." She paused to purse her lips. "Stop giving me that doubting look, girl, and just listen." She recited another spell. This time I recognized each word. There were only four of them, but I'd never heard them in this sequence before.

When it was my turn to recite what she'd said, I held the apple in both hands and pictured a generous wolf-sized bite taken out. Naturally, nothing happened. Not so much as a twitch, twinkle, or even a nudge within my body.

"You don't *believe* it's possible," Grandma said with a cheesy grin.

"I do."

"No, you don't." She poked the apple. "You see other spell-casters casting spells willy-nilly like your wizard friend and you think you don't have to work for it."

Grandma touched the center of her chest with her hand. "Look at me. I am a little old wolf at this point, but my belief is as vast as my beautiful homeland. Perhaps even more." She extended her hand, and I returned the apple. She brought the piece of fruit to her lips, mumbled the words again, then kissed it. She presented the apple, revealing a lipstick stain where the apple's red was now green. Whoa, now that was clever.

Grandma said, "This is a very powerful spell—if you do it right and don't use another living being as a source of power."

I grasped the stubborn apple again, imagining what I could do. After speaking the words again, the fruit refused to budge. A couple tries later and I still didn't make any progress.

"Be patient," she said with a soft smile. "Saint Peter's Basilica wasn't built in a day."

I nodded, imagining the wondrous things I could do when I was ready to do the impossible.

# CHAPTER THIRTEEN

Two days passed with little progress. I'd like to say that the calm in the deep woods had a way of easing my fears, but I woke up again that Wednesday morning with the sensation of beetles crawling up and down my back. I sat up, and Thorn's head rose.

"What is it?" He was immediately alert.

I swung my feet over the side of the full-size bed, grateful to feel my running shoes were where I'd left them. They were ready. Shoelaces undone. Bag nearby and barely unpacked.

"Just a bad dream," I lied.

"No more bad dreams." He reached for me and tried to tug me back to bed, but I refused. I ran my right hand along the warm spot where I'd slept, finding it bug-free.

Not long after waiting for others to shower—including Aunt Vera who took forever to wash her hair—I ended up at the breakfast table munching away. Since I had to sit, I used the time to piece things together. It didn't take me long to ponder on the universe: essentially, we still had *no* leads on where the werewolves went.

"I want you to rest today," Thorn said firmly. The look on his face meant business, but I had too much to do.

"We don't know where those two werewolves went, so I need to pound the pavement for a little while. Maybe see if any of the locals have any information."

"Do you think they'll speak to us? Wolves probably aren't popular around here."

"I don't have a choice."

Thorn reluctantly accompanied me into town. The area seemed quiet, yet less tranquil, compared to the last time we ventured into Stitchings. I scanned the faces of every driver who passed us, checking to see if I recognized any of them, but none of them appeared to be related to our suspects.

We checked the marina first, going from boat to boat to see if the werewolves had been here recently. A leprechaun, heading out to fish with his brother, had little news for us either.

"Can't say that I've seen any werewolves around these parts lately." He spat a ribbon of tobacco over the side of his tugboat. "If they've left town, it's for the best between you and me."

I thanked them—even after they scowled at me.

"We should check each farm around the lake," Thorn suggested.

I sighed, knowing the hours of work ahead, then I caught sight of a truck, pulling up to the grocery store. Owen got out and began the slow process of unloading supplies from the back.

Without another word, I hurried over to help.

"You've already done enough." He tried to shoo me away, but Thorn had already stacked up a hefty load. In three strides, my mate had carried it inside.

"We should do more." I took a couple more and followed Thorn.

"Say, I heard from Todd that you ended up over at his place," Owen said. "He sure is grateful you set him free."

"This whole situation is frustrating," I replied. "I came here to find the Seed Seller and discovered a lot more problems—including a powerful elf."

"That would be Calliope. I should've warned you about her. Gerhard had her brought in."

"Don't worry about that. How are you holding up?" I moved to help open the register, but he declined my help.

"So far I've been open for half-days," he explained. "At least until my nephew can drive up here from Long Island. He'll take over so I can take Patty's body to her sisters."

We stood in silence for a while. Thorn leaned against the wall nearby.

"Have you found anything?" he asked quietly.

"We're stuck. The werewolves left the Farrow place and we're not sure where they went."

Owen tapped the counter as if deep in thought. "I wish I knew more, but those bastards have hidden away. There're hundreds of acres of farmland and forest around here. They could be anywhere. If it helps though, last I heard the werewolves might be living out there in their RV. It's a pretty old Winnebago Chieftain. You can't miss it."

"Thanks," Thorn said. "Anything helps."

An idea came to mind. One I hadn't considered since the carnival. "Do you know anything about Granger Cranberries?"

"You must mean the old Granger farm. They had a nice place out near the bogs. It's rundown. The Grangers had to sell the place, but no one wanted to buy it. Might not hurt to see if those werewolves might be hiding out there."

"We should check it out after dinner tonight," I said.

"With reinforcements," Thorn added. "Do you think we can just show up and they'll admit they murdered Patty?"

I had a sinking feeling we'd have to take them by force.

"The only way to find out is to ask them." I tried to sound hopeful, but even I knew most cornered wolves bit first and asked questions later.

Even if the Stravinskys were on the run, birthdays were still celebrated. Instead of a mere celebratory dinner and a simple cake for my dad's birthday, Mom baked one of his favorite treats, a cherry pie. The thing bordered on dangerous with enough sugar to take out a borderline diabetic.

As the sun set, my family made additional party preparations: Aunt Vera's children strung up the Christmas lights we found in a box in the attic, and Uncle Boris took the outrageous speakers from the back of his van and hooked them up to play Russian party music. The rave lasted for twenty minutes before Mom put a stop to that.

Just like any other dinner, we gathered at the table, sang the birthday song, then we ate dessert for dinner.

After we decimated the angel food cake and the cherry pie, Mom said to me, "It's a shame we didn't have a rack of lamb for my Fyodor's birthday."

"We've passed farms," Aunt Vera said offhand. "I don't know why we didn't stop and get one."

I snorted. "Who in their right mind would let random strangers buy a lamb? We'd have to load it into your minivan too."

Aunt Vera, Aunt Olga, and Grandma turned to me in disbelief.

"Who said I meant *buy*?" Aunt Vera said with absolute seriousness. "I'd just take it."

Why couldn't I have a normal family?

Minus a succulent rack of lamb, we'd managed to eat until we were lazy and sated. Folks chatted quieted over hot tea. We watched regular TV now and then, so my parents had plenty to say about current events. Unfortunately, during our post-dinner conversations, Uncle Boris said the dreaded words, "You know nothing, Vera."

No one said a word as my aunt replied, "Do we need to hold a game of Trivial Pursuit? The Werewolf Edition?"

Even Grandma gasped.

Karey laughed and said, "I'm not playing. You guys never play fair."

"Never," Aunt Vera replied. "I play to win."

With those words said, Karey picked up Sveta and headed into the kitchen.

"Let's bake some banana bread for Grandpa," she said to her daughter. "I have a feeling we're gonna have some hungry people after this."

I caught the sounds of Karey fetching bowls and warming up the oven. I got up to help, but Thorn caught my arm.

"You're not abandoning me," he said with a chuckle. "I'm like Karey. I thought my father and Will were vicious during games, but your family is no joke."

I rolled my eyes as the teams were formed. Thorn, Dad and I would play against two other teams. Aunt Vera, Aunt Olga, and Mom formed the second team while Alex and Uncle Boris were the final one. Grandma sat on the sidelines to keep things fair. Each team sat on opposite sides of the living room. Uncle Boris glared at my aunt and slid his thumb across his throat. Aunt Vera bared her teeth at him.

"This time we won't be fighting," Dad warned.

Uncle Boris booed while Alex gave a thumb-down in protest.

Dad continued. "Each team gets one question. One. Then the other team will have sixty seconds to answer. Agreed?"

"I won't need a minute," Uncle Boris boasted. "But for my dear sister Vera, we shall give her a full minute. Elderly minds get slow after all."

My aunt kept a straight face and blew him a kiss.

"Since it's my birthday, I will go first with a question to my wife's family." Dad shifted to the all-women team. "In 1588, there was a werewolf captain who worked for the Queen of England. He intercepted the oncoming Spanish Armada and took out multiple ships. And yet, he was never rewarded, nor his all-werewolf crew. Who was it?"

Aunt Olga bit her lip as she concentrated, and Aunt Vera turned to Mom to whisper in her ear.

Meanwhile, Thorn asked me, "Have you heard of that guy?"

I shrugged. Thorn and I had attended the human schools and learned human history. Not that our elders didn't teach us about werewolves, only that we never got to these nitty-gritty, far-fetched facts.

Ten more seconds passed as Aunt Vera replied, "That would be Ashley Worth."

"Correct." Dad gave her a nod and slipped her a red checker chip he'd stolen from the checker box game in the corner.

"Took you long enough," Uncle Boris said.

"Oh, be quiet. Now it's my turn and my question is for you," she said.

Uncle Boris leaned forward, eager to show off. "During the American Revolution, which you probably witnessed, by the way, a werewolf helped clear the path for Paul Revere's ride. He intercepted two British soldiers who could have shot the man down. Who was it?"

The blank look on my brother's face said he had no idea. He glanced at Uncle Boris, who had the kind of focus you'd only see if he spotted a beautiful woman he wanted to talk to.

Dad glanced at his watch and amusement grew on his face as the seconds ticked by. Uncle Boris began to mumble, "It was. It was."

Aunt Olga grinned at Mom. "He doesn't know!"

"Who was it, Boris?" Aunt Vera asked sweetly.

"Oh, hush," my uncle said. "I know who it was. It was my good friend Bob Carrington."

I almost choked on my sip of water. Who the hell was *Bob Carrington*?

Uncle Boris kept going. Apparently, he liked putting on a show. "Robert Carrington, born 1758, was a trapper and a supporter of the Continental Army. When he heard Mr. Revere was making his run," he demonstrated by holding up his fingers to show a man running, "he ran through the woods and helped the cause."

Aunt Vera mumbled, "Correct."

"What was that?" Uncle Boris asked loudly.

"Correct," she said sharply.

Dad tossed a red poker chip and Alex caught it mid-air.

After a couple rounds, Aunt Vera was clearly the winner with a generous stack of seven red checkers, while Uncle Boris only had three. She wouldn't even let dad win on his birthday either. My team had only secured one checker, but at least our loss would have a sweet end. The heavenly scent of baking banana bread filled the entire house.

"Another round?" Uncle Boris asked.

Groans echoed all around the room, but Aunt Vera grabbed at Aunt Olga's arm before the woman could escape.

"Do you like punishment, my friend—" Aunt Vera began to say.

Suddenly, the back door slammed, and Karey strode into the room. Her pained gaze connected with Alex's and I knew what she'd say before she opened her mouth.

"What's wrong?" Mom stood.

"The trees have sent an urgent message," Karey said, clearly shaken. "The hound is on its way back to the last place you left it in Canada. And it's not alone. There are five of them now."

The oven dinged, a resounding roar in a dead, silent room.

# CHAPTER FOURTEEN

Under the cover of the night, Dad, Uncle Boris, Thorn, and I made our way toward the Granger farm. All around us, the Maine woods whispered secrets. The half-moon seemingly beckoned us to run instead of hunt.

The farm emerged from the darkness, an eerie silhouette against the night sky. According to my brief Internet search, this place once had vibrant cranberry fields. Now the farm was a tangled mess of weeds and decay. As we approached, the first thing that caught my eye was the broken-down sign hanging lopsidedly on one nail. The once-bold letters now were faded and read, "Granger Cranberries." The sign creaked ominously as a gentle breeze brushed past, a sorrow-laden sound that seemed to echo the farm's forsaken state.

"Did Owen say what kind of RV we're looking for?" Uncle Boris asked.

"He said it was an older model. A Winnebago Chieftain," I replied.

We crept our way deeper into the property and

approached the main house. Its windows were boarded up and grime streaked the surface.

Dad stopped suddenly. "Do you hear that?"

We listened, and sure enough, there were voices coming from the back of the house. We moved closer, staying hidden in the shadows.

When we reached the back, we spotted the RV in question—along with a woman and two men—arguing. They looked like average folks. One man was bald, while the woman had blue hair. The third, dark-haired fellow, towered over the others and was dressed in a black T-shirt and camo shorts. A downwind breeze crossed my nose, bringing their scent. We'd found the men who'd murdered Patty at the grocery store.

"Can anyone hear them?" I edged closer, fearful they'd catch our scent. "They're the ones we want."

"No," Dad said firmly. "The wind isn't our friend today."

But before we could learn more, the argument ended abruptly, and the trio disappeared into the house. I moved to go after them, but Dad grabbed my shoulder. He still averted his eyes out of respect for my position as alpha female.

"We have them," I hissed.

"We don't know what's in that house," Dad said firmly. "Work smarter, not harder, daughter."

We were so close. With a sigh, I followed the others back into the woods. We'd parked over a mile away. Once we were at a safe distance, my dad finally spoke again.

"Here's what I propose we do," Dad said with a look to Thorn for approval. "We're in their territory and we're at a disadvantage. I say we set a trap."

"How?" Thorn asked.

"Boris and I will scope out the property. When the time is right, we'll draw them out and lead them to that demon's boat," Dad explained.

Uncle Boris grinned. "Oh, this is gonna be fun."

"Why are you taking them to the night demon?" I folded my arms. "Why not the dryad?"

Dad snorted. "Those werewolves aren't gonna hang out and do gardening until justice is served. The night demon has the means to hold them until the local fae can deal with them."

I laughed a bit, imagining the madame swallowing those werewolves like finger sandwiches. "That idea might work."

"And you two," Dad said to Thorn and me, "will find the elf who beat up your uncle."

Uncle Boris grinned. "What a woman. Wait, why can't I help them?"

Dad continued and ignored his brother. "Our plan might not work if the elf is hunting for them. We need to intercept her and bring her to our side."

Thorn and I exchanged a glance. "That sounds easier said than done."

"She will not come willingly," I added.

"Then you need to persuade her." Dad chuckled a bit.

"Say we try that. We need to find her first," my mate said.

"We could use old magic," I replied.

Thorn's jaw twitched with irritation, but he reluctantly nodded. We'd reached the point where our complications were piling up and time wasn't on our side anymore.

With a plan in place, we split up. Uncle Boris and Dad returned to hide near the house while Thorn and I fled back to the car. The woods felt alive around us, every rustle of the leaves a potential threat. A bush jostled and I almost imagined a hellhound busting out like back in Central Park. I waited and listened.

"Smell something?" Thorn asked.

"Don't know. I'm twitchy at this point."

"Do you think this will work?"

"I hope so. I just know I don't wanna fight Calliope again."

A half hour later, we were deep in the woods north of Stitchings. Thorn was beside me, his amber eyes scanning the dense trees.

"Twenty square miles of forest, and we're looking for a needle in a haystack." Thorn muttered, his voice low.

I couldn't help but agree. The area was too vast, the task seemingly impossible. But we had no choice. Those werewolves would find the elf sooner or later.

I knelt, placing my hand on the cool, damp ground. Closing my eyes, I pictured her in my mind—the blonde hair, the black eyes, her sturdy build. I reached for the old magic and waited for the tug. It was like walking blindfolded on a tightrope over a chasm.

The magic surged, a wild, untamed force. I felt a sharp stab in my back, a reminder of the risks. I gasped as the pain radiated through my body.

"Easy," Thorn said, his hand on my shoulder. "Don't push too hard."

I nodded and gritted my teeth as I drew back a bit. The magic was a living thing, a serpent coiling around my senses. Slowly, I tugged at the threads of power, weaving them into a connection with Calliope. It was a painstaking process, each pull sending jolts of pain through me. Finally, I felt a faint tug.

"There," I finally whispered, my voice barely audible. "She's to the west."

We got in the car and hit the back roads. Another half hour passed, and we hit a couple of dead-end streets. Eventually, the signal grew stronger until we came upon a tiny house, trailer, and a Dodge truck nestled among the trees. It was a whimsical structure in the colors of greens, blacks, and blues. The classic A-frame house was small, yet inviting.

Thorn and I crept closer, our steps silent. There was no

sign of anyone outside, but the sounds emanating from within spoke of life—the clatter of pots and pans, and an off-key rendition of a Stevie Nicks classic.

"Think that's her?" Thorn whispered, his eyes fixed on the trailer.

"It's gotta be," I replied.

I scanned the home and considered our options. Back when I'd fought the Jackson pack, I'd had battle elves on my side. They were known for their formidable power. They'd only helped me at the time because the Jackson pack had kidnapped one of their own. Maybe I could use the same tactic with Calliope. Wasn't the enemy of my enemy my friend in this case?

We decided to wait and watch, settling into a comfortable position at a safe distance. As we observed, a strange pain flared up in my back, a tender spot that seemed to throb in time with my heartbeat. I winced, touching the area gently.

Suddenly, my phone vibrated in my pocket, a startling intrusion. The goblin blade jerked hard too. I reached for the phone, but before I could check the screen, a voice cut through the air.

"How did you find me?" It was Calliope standing behind us. Her eyes were narrowed.

"We're not here to fight," I began.

She held two swords and extended them in our direction. The metal gleamed in the moonlight.

Thorn and I scrambled to our feet, dodging her first swing.

"We just want to talk!" Thorn yelled, but she continued to attack us.

I ducked under a sweeping blade, feeling the whoosh of air as it passed inches from my head.

"Get out of here!" Thorn tried to push me away, narrowly avoiding a thrust.

"I'm not leaving you!" I shot back.

The elf was a whirlwind of motion, her swords a blur. I had to get the goblin blade without getting cut in the damn process.

My phone rang again. I bolted to the east and stole a glance at the screen. It was my mother. I ignored it. Now wasn't the time.

The phone rang again and again.

Thorn managed to wrangle the elf to the ground, so I retrieved the goblin blade. It shifted to become an iron bowie knife.

I glanced at her swords. Her weapons were *much* bigger.

"Really?" I said to the goblin blade. "That's it?"

I raced back into the fray, suddenly realizing that each time the phone rang, the call didn't click over to voicemail.

*Something was wrong.*

The phone rang and this time I picked up the call.

"Nat, it's the Jackson pack," Mom said, her voice trembling. "They're trying to get into the cabin."

I caught the thunderous rumble of doors breaking. "They know about your trap. They said they want the elf, or they'll hurt us."

My blood ran cold. "Mom, get out of there—"

On the other end of the line glass shattered, growls filtered through, then the phone went dead.

Calliope grinned and lowered her swords slightly. "Your pack betrays you," she said bitterly.

"They're not my pack." I met her heated gaze. "They're a threat to everyone."

Her smile shifted to a smirk. "Sure. If you say so."

"I don't have time for this," I hissed. "As much as I'd like to run in circles, my family needs me." I edged away and Thorn did the same. "My family arrived here a couple days ago.

Gerhard knows this. Since he hired you, you can confirm my story, right?"

Calliope took a step forward, then scowled as she hesitated.

"Call them," Thorn pressed, not taking his eyes off the elf. "Nat, run to the car."

I pivoted to run away, but when I turned, I discovered we weren't alone.

Eleven men emerged from the woods. All of them were armed with weapons and guns. I recognized the bald man from the back of house. How the hell did he find this place? A sinking feeling hit.

Damn, I'd led those werewolves straight to Calliope.

I'd like to say I'd gotten better at figuring out if I'd been followed, but apparently, I'd lost my edge. Even Thorn had been too busy to detect them. The eleven men advanced toward us. With my bad luck over the last couple of months, a hellhound was not far behind.

The air was thick with tension as the moonlight glimmered faintly off the surface of the nearby creek.

My clammy grip on the goblin blade faltered as the weapon extended into a silver-tipped spear. Beside me, Thorn's fists clenched. Even the elf couldn't wait to fight. The delight on her face bordered on manic.

The short, redheaded man holding the .45 smirked at us. "Long time no see, Stravinsky." His finger tightened on the trigger.

"Sorry to disappoint you, but I don't remember you," I murmured.

His smirk widened. "We were rather busy at the time. You and a bunch of your friends put up quite the fight that day."

"Jackson pack, right?" I couldn't resist adding, "Didn't you lose that day?"

Gun dude fired a single shot at my feet. I didn't flinch as a growl rumbled in Thorn's chest.

"Enough talk." Thorn lunged toward the gunman with a snarl. Gun dude barely had time to react as Thorn's hand clamped down on his wrist, twisting it violently. The gun tumbled to the ground. With a swift kick, Thorn sent the man sprawling into the tall grass.

The others charged. The first attacker came at me with a knife, slashing wildly. I parried with the shaft of my spear, then thrust the tip forward, catching him in the shoulder. He howled in pain, the sound abruptly cut off as I used the spear shaft to sweep his legs from under him.

Four couldn't wait to pounce on Calliope. She surged forward as her blades sliced through two of them. One of her opponents, a rather bold fellow with a machete, tried to get in a hit and she cleaved his blade in two. He took another look at her and bolted.

Not far from me, Thorn never stopped moving. He picked up another man and hurled him into the nearby creek. The poor man flopped about as his face scraped the rocky bottom. Another man came at Thorn and my mate ducked a wild swing. Then Thorn delivered a crushing blow to the man's stomach, followed by an uppercut that sent him flying.

Now there were three left.

A guy in a light green T-shirt approached me and bared his teeth. I pivoted to face him. Green shirt dude dodged my first swipe, but not fast enough to avoid my second jab. The goblin blade slid through his shoulder, eliciting a scream as the silver burned him.

The two remaining fellows hovered beyond reach. The confident smirks on their faces had melted away. Now they helped their fallen friends up and crept back—away from

Calliope. The elf motioned for them to attack her, but they shook their heads.

*Smartest move you've made today, boys.*

We watched them limp, scamper, and crawl away.

"Let's take them out so they don't follow us." She grinned with glee and stepped forward, but my hand rose.

"They're underlings," I said. "Let them go. The man behind all this has my family."

"So the fighting isn't over," she breathed.

"Not by even close," I replied.

After Calliope locked up her house and told Gerhard what was about to go down, we jumped in the SUV. None of us were hurt—which was good. They'd taken my family and I'd need every ounce of willpower I had to make them pay.

We made it halfway to our cabins before I got another phone call.

"Looks like you've been busy," a man with a deep voice said.

I put the call on speaker. "If you hurt them, I'll—"

"You'll fuck me up like you did my people?" the man grated. "Oh, no, you won't have the upper hand this time."

Thorn's grip on the steering wheel tightened.

"May ask the name of the asshole I'm speaking to?" I asked.

"Ernest is the name," the man replied. "You'll be hearing it when you come begging."

I rolled my eyes. "Sure."

Ernest added, "Come to the cranberry farm or I'll have to show you how I deal with people who can't mind their own business."

"Why should I just show up?" I bit out. "I want proof you have my family."

Ernest chuckled. "Sure. Why not?"

The sounds of Ernest's footsteps across a backyard deck bled through the phone, then I heard a grunt.

"Bring the blonde woman," he ordered.

A pained grunt came next. It was Mom. She'd likely been gagged.

"Did you hurt her?" My voice sounded unsteady as red-hot rage pulsed through me. I almost crushed my phone until Thorn reached over and squeezed my leg.

When I'd calmed down enough to speak, I said, "We're on our way."

"And the elf?" Ernest asked.

"I'm here," Calliope said from the backseat. "And I'm going to kill you," she added.

Ernest laughed. "I find that hard to believe since you never found us, but yeah, you can try to kill us, you elf bitch."

I hung up before his laugh made my ears bleed.

"Thank you," Thorn grated.

The car went quiet. All of us were trying to process not only what happened, but what would we do once we reached the cranberry farm.

"Do we have a plan?" I asked.

"Kill them?" Calliope asked with all seriousness.

"Naturally, but the minute we show up, they could shoot us. That dude with the .45 back there could be one of many. For all we know, they might have hunting rifles, or even automatic weapons. And it's obvious this is all a trap."

While I spoke, I shot off a message to Dad and Alex. They were supposed to be hanging out near the farm to drive the werewolves to the night demon. Usually, Alex was quick to reply, but I got nothing. Shit.

"I'll take care of the guns," Calliope said firmly. "Now that we know where those bastards are, the fairy folk are already heading over there. If Ernest wants a fight, he'll get one. I just need a diversion before they pull the trigger."

Thorn nodded.

"They will try to take your weapon," Calliope said to me. "Don't let them take your goblin blade."

I sighed. The goblin blade was horrible for covert transport. "How did you know what it is?"

I turned in the seat to see Calliope with folded arms and a smug smile on her face.

"A weaponsmith like myself appreciates a finely crafted blade," she replied. "You possess one of the few weapons crafted by the Great Moliner."

This was the first person who'd told me more information about my mysterious weapon. So far even Bill hadn't told me who had made it or where he'd gotten it from. For all I knew he'd probably swindled someone.

"I'll see if I can hide it," I said, "but it won't be too easy."

"It is easy." She leaned forward in the seat. "If you are its true owner, then you can tell it what to do…Sometimes."

I pulled up my pants leg. "Hey, goblin blade."

Nothing happened.

"It's not like those *fancy* speakers or phones," Calliope griped. "Tell it what you want, but you must have clear intentions. No doubts whatsoever."

"Move to the right," I said, adding authority to my words. The blade was quiet for a moment until it jostled against my leg. "Now disappear."

The goblin blade dematerialized, but when I reached for it, I could feel it attached to my leg. It would've been nice if Bill had told me about that.

Calliope nodded with approval. "Very good. Now's not a good time, but if we have a chance to sit and celebrate, I'll be happy to tell you more about your knife."

I gave her a nod, genuinely hoping we'd have an opportunity to celebrate.

Fifteen minutes later, we pulled up on the road outside of the cranberry farm.

"Should we sneak over there, or do we have to present ourselves?" I asked.

"I suspect if we don't show up, they'll harm your family," Calliope said.

"I agree," Thorn said. "I don't like the idea of walking in when they can simply execute us, but for now, they have the upper hand."

So we drove into the farm's parking lot, taking our time. Ernest's men waited for us. I didn't recognize any of them. A tall man wearing a camouflage T-shirt and jeans directed us to park behind two other utility vehicles. Thorn did as instructed, and we got out with our hands raised. One thing I noticed immediately was Calliope didn't have a single sword on her. The tall werewolf even patted her down, checking her jeans pockets and grabbing her in places that no man should touch. The elf didn't twitch, but the moment the man backed away, her eyes formed slits, and I knew that tall wolf would be one of her first targets.

"This way," the man said.

One of the men pointing .45s at us barked out, "Go ahead and try something. These bullets are capped with silver. I got shot with one of these the other day, and I guarantee you won't live with one of these puppies in your head."

"Yeah, yeah." Thorn jerked his head for us to follow them.

I scanned the abandoned lot that we'd visited no more than a couple of hours ago. There were far more cars here now and the scent I'd caught around Patty's body filtered through. These were the people we were looking for.

Tall dude and two other men led us into the house. The 1940s farmhouse had seen better days with its chipped paint and barely hanging screen door. The inside was stuffy and stank of unwashed clothes and food left out too long. We marched through the house and left through the back to the deck. A couple hours ago, we'd watched those two men and that woman stand here. They'd put on quite the show once they knew we'd found them. I should've known the moment we walked on the property that we could've been followed.

Those three werewolves sat on lawn chairs, two of them gabbing as if we'd walked in on a cookout. The man in the middle was a lewd-looking fellow with slicked back dirty blonde hair, and a leader's calm expression. The woman to his left was lanky with sharp green eyes and dyed blue hair. The third bald fellow, whose ass we'd kicked not too long ago, appeared far more submissive. He had quite a grisly looking head injury, yet he still nodded, and only spoke when the other two finished.

Meanwhile, my family was hogtied to the ground, bound with silver-lined ropes. I checked their faces: Dad, Mom, Aunt Olga, Uncle Boris, Aunt Vera, her children, and Grandma. No Alex or his wife and child. Had they gotten out in time?

I must've stopped, for one of our guards shoved me in the back to push me forward. "Keep moving, dammit."

Just seeing Grandma with a handkerchief stuffed in her mouth and her hands and feet bound tapped into the rage I'd smoothed.

"Not now," Thorn mumbled.

The man sitting in the central chair said, "Yes, Natalya, now isn't the time for your bravery." I connected the voice to the name as Ernest gestured to my family. "We could've killed any of them, but they aren't who we want." Ernest eyed Calliope and his grin widened.

He said to her, "After your people cursed my brother

Graves, I made sure they got what they deserved. But then you had to show up and kill Graves."

Calliope reflected his sinister smile. "You talk about people minding their own business. Graves was cursed for a reason. He stalked and killed one of our younglings, so I slit his throat."

Ernest shot to his feet. "Do not speak my brother's name, elf bitch."

"You should've kept your family in line," Calliope bit out. "The fairies around here wouldn't have called me in from the Old Lands unless he'd broken the peace."

Ernest's stony face said far more than words. He didn't care what his brother had done or the consequences—only that he wanted to settle the score.

"One death leads to another and another," I said softly. "Did you really think that you could kill off the fairies without them striking back?"

Ernest took a swig of his cheap beer and slowly placed it back in the holder on his lawn chair. "I assumed those backwoods fairies would know better than to cross my pack. They paid the price and, after we kill you and the fairies' hired gun, we'll ride en masse through this whole fucking town and kill them all. This ends now."

Ernest's boast hung in the air and somehow left a foul odor under the layers of rot on the farm. The urge to check to see if reinforcements were coming grew overwhelming. Calliope had asked for a diversion, but the three of us had at least five guns trained on us. Did she expect one of us to bolt?

The head honcho flicked his ringed fingers in Calliope's

direction. "Kill her last. I want to enjoy watching her suffer. Just get rid of the others."

"No!" Thorn took a step forward and gun dude pressed the muzzle against my mate's gut.

"Don't think about it, motherfucker," the man spat.

"What is there to talk about?" Ernest got up and threw his empty beer can into the field of broken-down vehicles and farm equipment. I could have sworn that I saw a tiny head shoot down. Had the fairies arrived?

Ernest continued. "Do you want to pick your gravesite?"

"You sound like a man willing to barter for the right price," Thorn said smoothly. His fingers slowly opened and closed. I'd never seen my mate do that before. Was he trying to signal someone? "You ultimately want to clear the deck, as they say. Let me kill the elf and you set my family free."

My head shot in Thorn's direction. Had he lost his natural mind? Even worse, Thorn hadn't lied. His scent didn't betray his words.

Ernest chuckled. "Well, you are the hero, or maybe I should say, the executioner. Where do you come from, friend?"

"South of here, in Jersey."

"Pack leader, eh?"

"Yeah, and I plan on getting back to my pack one way or another. If I have to kill this so-called 'elf bitch' to return safely, then so be it."

Ernest settled back into his seat and the blue-haired wolf beside him scowled.

"What makes you think you can trust him?" the woman snapped. "We don't know him."

"Oh stop, Seraphina," he replied. "I don't care who he is as long as he kills the elf."

"Do I have your word that you'll set everyone free after I snap her neck?" Thorn took a step toward Calliope, and this time I wasn't mistaken. The beer can Ernest had thrown shifted ever so slightly as if an unseen hand moved it. I didn't smell any fairies nearby, though.

Thorn sidestepped and stood behind the elf. They were practically the same height. My mate placed his hands around her neck.

Calliope raised her chin in the air. "This changes nothing," she warned. "If you kill me, more hired fighters will come. Do you want—"

"Oh shut up!" Seraphina barked. "Enough of the talking. Turn around and face your killer," she purred. "I want you to see the look on his face when he ends your life."

Thorn's jaw twitched, and I prayed that whatever happened, he wouldn't feel guilty for this. The moment his grip tightened, the back of one of the rusty trucks in the parking lot jostled then rolled our way. Shouts rang out, and the surrounding wolves scrambled.

"What the fuck?" Bald man shouted.

The rusted cranberry tractor shook violently, then shot out toward Ernest and Seraphina. Bald dude simply stood there, his mouth opening wide as the cranberry tractor plowed through him. Seraphina and Ernest leapt out of the way. The armed henchman opened fire. Bullets pelted the oncoming vehicles, but no one drove them.

Seeing an opportunity, I bolted to my father. The moment I reached for his silver ties, the magic in them tightened and my father grunted in pain.

"Sorry. Sorry I'll get them off." I lifted my pants leg and said firmly, "Time to get to work. I need a cutter."

The goblin blade materialized as Calliope had promised. As soon as I pulled it out of the holster, the goblin blade shifted until it became a pair of handheld bolt cutters. The tool sliced through the ropes with ease. As I jumped from person to person to set everyone free, Thorn and Calliope kept the werewolves occupied.

The bloodhungry elf had slipped off her belt buckle, and the sliver of metal had transformed into a blade attached to the end of the long leather strap. She whipped the strap back and forth, twirling it in the air. It struck Seraphina and knocked the wolf off her chair. She flopped to the ground, clearly knocked out cold.

Ernest picked up one of his fallen comrade's guns and fired widely. One shot clipped me in the leg. I fell hard. Another bullet hit my father in the shoulder as he attempted to protect Mom and Grandma.

The searing pain from the silver-tipped bullet burned and spread down my leg. I staggered, but I managed to get back up. Pain be damned, I'd had enough.

Once I'd freed everyone, the goblin blade lengthened to a spear again. Time to end this. I leapt through the air and threw it toward Ernest. The spear hit Ernest's gun with a loud *clang*, then struck Ernest in the face with a hard thud. He collapsed to the ground.

With the leader down, the sentient equipment around us shuttered to a stop, and the farm fell silent. Bodies lay everywhere. Each of the shooters had been mowed down, but Seraphina and Ernest had somehow made it through this with their lives.

# CHAPTER SIXTEEN

With little time left to fulfill Hyacinth's deal, we raced to *The Gray Glen* with a tied-up Ernest and Serafina in the back of Thorn's SUV. The sun would rise soon. My mate drove at breakneck speed while I sat in the front, my gaze set to the faint glow growing to the east.

Calliope sat in the backseat with her sword stretched across her lap. Even though our enemies were tied up, the elf held her sword like an old friend waiting for the next dance.

We weren't the only ones in the car. Uncle Boris had insisted on coming and sat opposite the elf. He stared at her adoringly. The elf had yet to turn in his direction or say anything. I had the mind to warn her about my uncle later, but she'd likely already smelled his horrid aftershave.

"Any word yet from Alex and his family?" Thorn asked me.

"Nothing yet," I replied. "Dad texted me not too long ago. He said my aunts and cousins are out in the woods searching for them."

He briefly squeezed my hand to reassure me.

The horizon continued to lighten up, going from deep purple to a light pink. Our time was running out.

"Drive faster," I urged.

"I'm going eighty," Thorn growled, "but I can't drive like this on these winding roads."

Finally, we reached the visitor lot outside of the reserve. A barricade prevented our entry.

Thorn cursed. "Park's closed."

"Doesn't matter." I got out. "I'll drag both of them in if I have to."

I popped open the back. I grabbed Serafina's leg, but Calliope had quickly gotten out of the car and stopped me with a hand on my shoulder. "You're hurt. I got her."

"Don't you touch me," Seraphina growled.

The elf tugged her out with far too hard of a pull, then Calliope hefted the woman over her shoulder. Ernest merely glowered at Thorn as my mate grabbed him. After that, it turned into a race as we ran through the forest. No matter how badly my leg screamed for me to stop, I ran faster.

"How much time until sunrise?" Calliope asked.

"Don't ask," Thorn said. "Just keep going."

The moment I spied the three hills in the distance, my heart soared. I'd made it—somehow. Those five days had passed far too quickly. I hurried as fast as I could and ignored the pain. With every step, the bullet embedded in my leg sang. When I reached the glen, I collapsed from exhaustion.

Not far from me, Hyacinth had already started packing. The clothesline was gone, as well as the rain barrel. The sprouts in her garden had grown into full crops. A nearby wheelbarrow and basket blurred as if they were winking out of existence.

Uncle Boris swept me into his arms. "Just a couple more steps."

He carried me up the hill—right as the dryad stepped out of her shop. As my uncle put me down, I gave her a nod, and she repeated the gesture.

"Glad to see you, Wolf," she said with a soft grin.

Thorn and Calliope unceremoniously dumped the goods on the ground. Instead of asking for the seed, I had another question.

"What will you do with them?" I asked.

The side of Hyacinth's mouth tilted up into a smirk. "They're coming with me to Yakutia. The cold weather may change their malevolent moods."

"Are you going to kill them?"

"Does that matter?"

After everything I'd experienced the last couple of months with Bill, Rex, and now this mess in Maine, I had a distinct answer. "Yes, it does. What they did to Patty and the other fae was unthinkable but killing them won't bring her back."

"No, it won't." She motioned for me to come inside.

"What about them?" I jerked my chin toward Ernest and Serafina.

She disappeared inside and threw over her shoulder, "I won't kill them—yet."

I limped into the shop's cool interior. Even in here, the dryad had made preparations for travel. She'd stacked many of the barrels of goods against a far wall.

"Have a seat." She pointed to a stool next to her counter.

Hyacinth fetched this and that from her jars of herbs and seeds. Using a mortar and pestle, she fashioned a poultice with a splash of water.

"Do you have time to do that?" I asked. "Don't you need to leave soon?"

"No, no." She applied the poultice to a bandage, then stooped before me. "This is my domain. I have enough power to hold the door open once in a while." She even winked at me.

"Then we still had time left," I breathed. "That's a relief."

She snorted, quite the funny sound with her high-pitched voice. "Actually, you're a half hour late, but technically you did capture Ernest before the sun rose."

I frowned. At least the effort counted.

The dryad lifted my bloodied pants leg and examined my wound. "You endured a lot to help us."

"It looks worse than it feels. You don't have to help." My body was already trying to push the bullet out, but it would take time.

Her dark eyebrow rose. She didn't believe my lies one bit. "I'm sure it doesn't hurt, but it's best for you to avoid an infection."

"Excuse me?"

She applied the poultice to the bullet wound and flashed me a knowing grin again. "Just be quiet and let someone help you, Natalya Stravinsky. You need all the help you can get." She slipped her hand into her apron pocket and pulled out a folded piece of paper.

"What's this?" I asked as she placed it in my hand.

"Your prize. It will summon a dragon."

I opened the dark yellow parchment to reveal a shiny green seed. It was far too light to hold something as majestic as a dragon. I tilted it and the lantern light in the room reflected off it.

"What do I do with it?" I blurted out.

She pursed her lips as if I should know. "Plant it?"

"Are you serious? The hellhounds are searching for me. I don't have the years—or even months to wait for this to grow."

She must've read the rising panic in my expression, for she reached forward and grasped the side of my face with her warm palms. "You've come this far, Natalya. Plant this in a place where the warmth in your heart shines the brightest, and your champion will come to you."

"But?"

"No but." She lifted my chin, forcing me to stand.

This time my leg supported me with ease. "How did you do that? I don't feel the bullet anymore."

"No, you don't feel it anymore because it's gone," she said with a knowing hum. "Guess I *know* what I'm doing."

I sighed and smiled. "Yes, you do. Thank you for everything." With those parting words, I bid her goodbye.

After climbing off the three hills, the four of us waited until The Gray Glen shimmered and was whisked away to Siberia.

# CHAPTER SEVENTEEN

With the hellhounds hundreds of miles away, yet closing in, my family gathered in one cabin. Thank goodness my aunts had found Alex, Karey, and Sveta hiding away in the woods.

When I'd returned to the cabins, my brother had explained what happened.

"Once I heard the killers coming, I grabbed them and ran," my brother had said with his head hung low. "I should've stayed and defended the pack—"

"You did well," Thorn had told him. "You were surrounded and outnumbered. Your family should come first."

Now that everyone was back together, we had a new mystery to uncover: *what the hell do we do with the seed?*

Not long after my dad lay down to rest, my mother, grandma, aunts, and uncle crammed themselves into the small kitchen and stood around the kitchen table. Everyone stared at the tiny seed settled on a glass saucer.

"Has it moved yet?" Aunt Vera whispered.

"Is it supposed to move?" Uncle Boris asked.

"Why are we whispering?" my mom added, clearly annoyed.

"I dunno," Uncle Boris said. "It's a dragon. Should we set it on fire?"

All heads snapped in his direction. I slid the seed closer to me.

"Are you serious?" Aunt Vera hissed. "Sure, let's toss it in the fireplace and burn your niece's only chance of survival!"

Uncle Boris ambled away. "I'm gonna go see what the elf is doing in her little happy house."

After we'd returned to the cabins from the reserve, the elf had set up camp with her tiny house on the other side of the pond.

Before the day was over, I'd have to have a little chitchat with my uncle about the elf. Now wasn't the time though. The Stravinsky women were huddled in the kitchen trying to figure out how to summon the champion.

"Should we grab one of those cracked pots in the front yard, some soil, and plant that sucker?" Aunt Vera asked.

"That sounds too easy," Mom said.

"Did the dryad give you specific instructions?" Grandma asked.

I told the others how the dryad wanted me to plant it in the place where the warmth of my heart shines the brightest.

Aunt Olga and Aunt Vera shared disgusted faces.

"Whatever does that mean?" Aunt Olga asked. "That sounds all flowery and such. No pun intended."

"Could it be literal?" Mom rubbed the side of her face, clearly tired after everything that had happened.

"Oh, Anna. I've yet to see Natalya's heart shine anywhere."

"I think it means she should plant this in the place where she's happiest," Mom suggested.

I chuckled. If that was the case, every store within fifty miles of this place was fair game.

"That sounds too easy, doesn't it?" Aunt Olga's beautiful face fell.

Now that I thought about it, I was happiest back home, the one place where I didn't want to go with the hounds on my heels.

Mom said no more and began packing up.

"Mom." I trailed after her as she grabbed the loaves of bread and added them to a plastic bag. "Why don't we just do as Aunt Vera suggested and put it in a pot in the backyard?"

Mom continued to stowaway the piles of groceries. Aunt Vera hurried over to help. Aunt Olga followed.

The decision to return to South Toms River spread through the cabins far faster than when I'd first made the difficult decision to leave.

Poor Dad still dealt with his wounds, but the overall mood in the cabin was lighter as we crammed our stuff into all the cars.

"Any idea where hellhounds are?" I asked Karey as we loaded our final things, our suitcases, into the back of Thorn's SUV.

"They're over a thousand miles away. Give or take. An elm mentioned something about a nearby lake with many islands."

"We looked that up," Alex said, "and it looks like the hellhounds are around Lake Nipigon in Ontario."

"That's still pretty far from us." Thorn patted my shoulder.

"Not far enough." I closed the SUV's rear hatch. "Thanks, Karey."

My sister-in-law gave me a quick hug. "The sooner we return home, the sooner we can plant the seed."

Other goodbyes needed to be said, so I trudged around the pond and found Calliope sitting on the narrow back stoop of her tiny home.

She wasn't alone.

Uncle Boris leaned against the side of the place with a relaxed expression.

"Hey, Calliope!" I called out.

The elf gave me a curt nod.

"We'd heading out in a bit," I said. "I just wanted to thank you for everything. For helping us take down Ernest and such."

"We had the same goal," she replied stiffly. "It was easy."

I snorted. "Didn't seem easy to me. You can stay here until Sunday. I booked the property for the entire week."

"Thank you," she replied. "It's very pleasant here."

"Heading back to Europe?" I asked.

"No, she's staying here," Uncle Boris said smoothly. "And I'm staying with her."

"What?" The sound floated out of my mouth, not as a question, but more in disbelief. I glanced at straight-faced Calliope, then my enamored uncle. I waited for Calliope to say something, but she didn't.

"The hellhounds are coming," I said to my uncle. "If you and Calliope plan to stay for a spell, then you should be careful."

"Let them come," Calliope said with absolute delight. "I can slow them down. Give them a chew toy."

"The hellhounds aren't coming for you, Callie," Uncle Boris said gently.

I sighed. "Are you sure you want to stay? You might end up killed if you're between them and me. If you need some cash, I have it. You can go someplace safer."

She shook her head. "I live to fight, Natalya. It's in my blood—just like your uncle." The elf smiled a bit, which revealed a hint of the dimples in her cheeks. "At first, I thought he was an idiot, but he used to be quite the soldier.

Even better, this morning he gave me something I haven't had in decades—"

Whoa there. "I don't need to know your personal business," I blurted out. He could've given her fresh flowers or something, but I still didn't wanna know. "Umm, just let me know if you need anything."

I hugged my uncle, not minding his overwhelming cologne this time. God knew I didn't want it to be the last time I smelled it.

"I'll be fine." He leaned down and kissed the top of my head. "This relationship isn't what you think it is, I promise."

The pensive look on his face made me pause. Was this the same man who'd spent his evenings in bars hunting women? Guess I'd have to find out when we crossed paths again.

I honestly believed we would.

~

For the many hours I stared at the rolling countryside, I checked every horticulture website I could get my hands on. Naturally, not a single one had an entry for a great dragon-summoning seed. Time to text the cavalry. I shot a text to Brenna asking if the earth witch had any intel on the seed.

"Are you sure you still want to see Dr. Frank before we go home?" Thorn asked as we drove through New Haven, Connecticut.

"I wanna go straight home, but I need to stop trying to figure everything out on my own." It was Friday, and my therapist's office was open. "The receptionist told me he'd squeeze me in."

"I think we're past wizards saving the day." My mate's voice sounded weary.

I smiled, thinking of how many times my good friend

Nick had helped me. "Dr. Frank is actually quite powerful. He doesn't have to save the day, but if he knows how to make this seed grow—or if he knows someone who can help—it will be worth the hour or two we lose."

Our trip heading south down I-95 took us through northern Manhattan, so we veered deeper into the city while my family continued to Jersey.

Twenty minutes later, Thorn dropped me off and I ran up the steps to Dr. Frank's Midtown office.

The receptionist behind the check-in desk grinned at me. Without making a phone call or sending a text—gotta love magic—she told me, "Dr. Frank has been waiting for you. Go head on in."

Across from the small waiting area, I spied the mahogany door to his office. I'd been here before many times over the years, and yet I'd never borne the weight of worries as heavy as I did now.

I walked in. Dr. Frank had a corner office—even though his office was in the middle of the building, and his space boasted quite the view of the Hudson River. (Even though the building was closer to the East River, but I digress.)

I sat in the familiar leather seat while a smiling Dr. Frank assessed me.

His gray eyes softened. "I wish we were seeing each other under better circumstances."

"I do too." I glanced around and inhaled the comforting smell of the leatherbacks in the bookcase behind him.

We'd held many one-on-one sessions here for my CBT, or Cognitive Behavior Therapy. Thanks to him, I'd confronted many of my obsessions head-on and learned to avoid my compulsions.

"How are things going with you-know-who?" he asked.

Dr. Frank didn't have to say her name. We both knew what he meant.

"Not well." The last time I'd seen him, I was freed from Diana and I was dealing with the leprechaun. Briefly, I told him about my trip to Maine.

The white-bearded wizard leaned forward and laid his clasped hands on his desk. "So much has happened to you. Before we talk about her, I want to ask how *you're* doing."

I couldn't resist laughing. We hadn't conducted a private session in a while, and I could tell that he could see every widening crack in my head. Back when I was a teenager, I'd sat in this same seat. Told every lie to get everyone to ignore my little collecting habit, and yet Dr. Frank saw through me. And he'd *helped* me.

So why did my maniacal laughter turn into sobs after such a simple question?

I glanced around, hoping my pent-up anxiety would retreat, but it bubbled forth and swallowed me whole. I cried, letting the emotions I'd held back burst forth. I wasn't sure how long I wept—only that Dr. Frank was genuinely concerned for me.

Once I quieted, it was my therapist who broke the silence. "I'm glad you came to see me. You've faced a lot of adversity lately and your resolve has been tested, hasn't it?"

"That and much more." I couldn't resist checking my watch.

"Don't worry about the time." He pointed to the window to his left.

I checked outside. To my surprise, a nearby pigeon was frozen mid-air.

"Did you seriously stop time?" I asked.

"Oh, no. I can't do that." He rubbed his beard with a small smile. "But I can *bend* time a little bit while we're in this office. The bird's moving, but relative to it, we're moving very fast."

He was right. The bird crept forward, inch by agonizing inch.

Dr. Frank continued. "Your final struggle is still coming. You'll be tested in ways you've never been tested before."

I harrumphed. "Can I skip that exam?"

"I wish I could take your place."

I instantly thought of Mevelyn. "Someone else already did. It's time for me to face Diana's hellhounds on my own." I reached into my pocket and pulled out the seed. "Do you know anything about the Seed of the Fates?"

He appeared serious, then his face softened. "I haven't seen one of those in a very long time. It was back in Europe and that particular seed didn't look as spry as yours. The man who owned it had to contend with a sea monster, but he never used his."

"Why not? Did the seed fail to grow?"

Dr. Frank glanced out the window and the summer sun revealed the wrinkles forming on his brow.

"He never got a chance to summon the dragon, did he?" I managed to ask.

"No, he did not survive, I'm afraid."

Icy fear settled in my stomach and grew. Why hadn't I pressed the dryad harder for instructions?

"Then I'm gonna need to find another way to drive away Diana's hounds." I sighed. "Other than the thrill of the hunt, I still don't understand why she'd bother with somebody like me. Doesn't she have mythical monsters and stuff that would be way more *interesting*?"

Dr. Frank's white eyebrows rose with amusement. "You don't give yourself enough credit, Natalya. You're something she doesn't encounter often."

"What's that?"

"You're a survivor."

He had a point there.

"You're the epitome of the clever underdog who keeps evading death," he said. "Like me, Diana can see how *strong* you are."

My therapist's words should've filled me with hope, but now that I sat here, I could only see the old Natalya. The one who'd sat alone in her house with no mate, no family, and no hope at getting over her mental illness.

"You are strong," he repeated. Then he reminded me of how I'd crossed the Atlantic Ocean to save Thorn from his death curse. He reminded me of the lengths I'd taken to find the Basilisk King. And he reminded me how I was willing to sacrifice my life for my family. For friends and strangers alike.

He continued. "When all of this is over, you and I must meet for a couple of one-on-one counseling sessions. I mean it. You've been through a great deal of trauma, and you haven't had the chance to process everything."

Reluctantly, I nodded.

"This goes against my usual policies, but do you mind if I reach out to your peers? At the last meeting, everyone asked about you."

I'd been too busy to attend. And when I did go, I had much bigger problems than my mental health. "You can tell them what's going on, but I don't want to worry them. They've helped me enough as it is."

"Natalya, that's what friends *do* for each other. That's what you've done for them when they're in need."

"True." I stood. As much as I wanted Dr. Frank to stretch out time for a year or two, it was time to go.

"Farewell and good luck." He inclined his head. "Oh, and one more thing."

"Yes?"

"If I don't hear from you in a month about an appointment, I'm coming down to Jersey to fetch you myself."

I sighed. There'd be no escaping from that clever white wizard. Dr. Frankenstein was *still* that good.

A little lighter on my feet, I left the office and Thorn picked me up.

The rest of the ride home was sobering.

Less than an hour later, we stopped at a gas station and Thorn checked to see if I'd heard anything from Brenna or found some intel on the seed.

"No word from Brenna and I've found nothing." I wanted to bang my head against the dashboard. That would probably be more useful at this point.

"Why don't we plant it in our backyard?" he suggested.

"And have a huge-ass dragon sprout up where our neighbors can see?"

"Good point. Guess we'll have to think of something once we get home?"

Hearing the word "home" eased the tension in my shoulders. The final fight was coming, but at least I'd do it among family and friends.

# CHAPTER EIGHTEEN

Since we hadn't been gone long enough to rent out our house, we moved back in that evening without a problem. Naturally, Thorn and I didn't want to escape, but we were ready to make a quick getaway again.

Before I even set foot in the house, I snagged a worn *Santa's Little Helper* flowerpot from the shed. After Thorn accidentally dropped it and cracked the side, I'd hidden it away. Now the little guy had a second chance to make a big impact. To add a bit of holiday cheer, I even wrapped a red ribbon around the rim and arranged the pot to get the best exposure when the sun rose tomorrow morning.

Less than an hour later, Thorn and I crashed hard on sleeping bags. We didn't have any beds yet since they'd been stuffed into the trailer, but we'd deal with that later.

After a dreamless night, I woke all alone the next morning feeling stiff and drained.

Just another day fighting rogue werewolves.

While I'd drooled on my pillow, Thorn had run to the groceries store for supplies. When he returned, he joined me in the kitchen.

"Whatcha got?" I asked as he unloaded a single sack.

"Just the basics," he replied. "Enough to make sandwiches and some drinks."

I opened the fridge and spotted a sad container of ketchup and a questionable bottle of milk. "We can fill up the fridge when this shit is over."

He emptied the bag, then spied my handiwork with the flowerpot. "Looks nice, but didn't you want it somewhere outside?"

"Yeah, I'm moving it tonight," I replied. "It's best to get whatever magic its got going as soon as possible."

"You hear from Brenna yet?"

I scratched the back of my head. "She got back to me last night after we fell asleep. She's gonna need some time to figure it out."

He slipped his arms around my waist and I rested the back of my head against him. His steady heartbeat thrummed and my fast beating one matched his.

"We'll be fine," he murmured. "You'll be fine."

The cellphone in Thorn's back pocket rang, but he ignored it.

"Nice and *quiet* now," he said drily.

"Too quiet." I couldn't resist smiling.

"Yeah, I almost got used to hearing those shows playing on the TV all the time."

"And your Russian is getting better, too," I reminded him.

"Language immersion for the win. Still can't speak well, but I've picked up enough to understand most conversations."

His phone rang again as I turned around to face him and we shared a delicious kiss. Now that we were alone again, I looked forward to doing more than cuddling if possible.

When I pulled back, Thorn said, "That was nice."

"We can do more of that tonight, but—"

"We have too many things to do."

For the third time, his phone went off.

"Are you gonna answer that?" I almost snuggled against his chest but thought better of it and added space between us.

"It's my dad." Thorn reached into his pocket and returned the call.

Within moments, Farley's voice jumped out. "I've been trying to call y'all all morning," he grumbled.

"Dad, I told you I'll be over there soon." Thorn rubbed the back of his head.

I couldn't resist smiling. Farley had quite a way with words, yet Thorn and his dad managed well enough.

"Is Natalya coming over, too?" Farley asked. "I can hear somebody breathing nearby. You two still in bed—"

"No!" we both blurted at the same time.

I added, "I need to stop by The Bends to see if Bill or anyone else knows about the seed, then I plan to stop by."

"Sounds good then." Farley cut off the call.

When I caught Thorn's exasperated expression, I couldn't resist a giggle. "Sounds like he's doing just fine."

"He's fine. Say, can you wait for me to go with you?" he asked.

"Time's not on my side right now. How about we meet at his place afterward?"

"I don't like you traveling alone."

"It won't be for long. At the first sign of danger, we're out of here again."

He appeared to hesitate, but I grabbed the keys to my Nissan Altima and the flowerpot. Time to escape.

"I'll be there soon," I threw over my shoulder.

It felt damn good to ride through town again, but I remained vigilant, checking around every corner. With the time I had in town today, there were a couple folks I wanted to check on.

It didn't take me long to get to The Bends. The store had opened about an hour ago, and half the lot was full of Saturday shoppers hungry for a deal.

The promotional sign I'd made for the Christmas in July sale was still up on the lawn. Last year when we'd done this, we'd gotten far more sales than the other stores in the area. Even into Labor Day. Folks just liked the word *sale*, I guessed.

I parked the car, wondering if I'd waltz in again, and find out that Bill was yet again nowhere to be found. But I was surprised when I strode into the back office and ran into not only my former employer, but Erica, and even our necromancer janitor, Quinton. A week ago, when I was trying to wrap up working for Seamus the leprechaun, our goth janitor had taken a leave of absence for his honeymoon. He hadn't stated when he'd return though. Did that mean that Rex didn't work here anymore? It would be a shame since his family needed the money.

"What are you doing here, Nat?" Erica asked with the tilt of her head. She even eyed the cheerful flowerpot in my hands. "You tackling some light gardening today?"

"You could say that." I put the flowerpot on Bill's desk.

"If that's a gift from your little trip to Maine," Bill said, "I prefer cash."

I rolled my eyes. "This is going to save me from Diana and her hounds."

Bill peered at it, even briefly taking off his glasses. Erica picked up the pot, tilted it this way and that, and even poked the soil.

"Does it start kicking some ass when Diana shows up?" Erica asked.

"That's what I came here to ask you, Bill." I got them

caught up on what happened in Maine. Bill kept a straight face through his glamour while Erica's mouth dropped open.

"You had to do *all* that for some itty-bitty seed?" Erica said.

"Pretty much," I said. "Have you ever heard of The Gray Glen or the Seed of the Fates?"

"I've heard of that dryad's store," Bill replied, "but I've never been out that way. From what I've heard, she doesn't frequent the cities. And the seed?" He lifted one of his shoulders in a shrug. "That's the kind of merchandise I don't mess with. And I can't believe you were just driving around town with something so valuable. What if someone takes it?"

Somehow, I held back a laugh. "Whoever wants to take it can get in line behind the hellhounds. I was hoping that you knew how to grow this thing. Do you have any contacts who might have more information?"

"I can ask around, but it won't be cheap."

"Then I'm sure you won't mind doing it as a *free* favor for me." I emphasized the word "free." These days, I was tired of being indebted to people.

"I can check, but it'll probably be the lowly, underhanded folks," Bill said.

I snorted. "Aren't those the *only* kind of people that you associate with?"

Quinton finally ambled over with the trash cart, bringing his death tomb fragrances of frankincense and myrrh. "What's that you got there? Did I hear you say it's a Seed of the Fates?"

"Yeah, it's a pretty fancy seed, but I have no idea how it works," I said. "Do you know anything about it?"

He briefly closed his midnight eyes as he considered the question. "I've heard of it, but I've never come across one."

I nodded. "Shouldn't you be on your honeymoon?"

After I said the question, Erica flashed me a you-shouldn't-have-asked-that look, and she darted away to go work at a nearby workstation.

Quinton said, "I wish I could've returned here on better terms, but things haven't gone well. My lovely lady decided to end our marriage not long after we'd arrived at Niagara Falls."

"I'm so sorry about that," I said to him softly.

For the next ten, I repeat, *ten* minutes, Quinton went into excruciating detail as to why his ex-wife had left him. Apparently, one of his zombie minions had walked in while the two of them were consummating their marriage. The zombie didn't want to share his master and showed up at the bridal suite with a box of condoms. Couldn't have little necromancers running around on his watch.

While Quinton spoke, Bill simply sat there enjoying my antics as I tried to gnaw my arm off to escape. I'd picked up the flowerpot and edged away. Pulled out my phone to see if someone needed me right away. I even tried to interrupt with advice, but Quinton just kept trucking along, barely taking a breath until he wrapped up with, "We've decided not to be friends either, but she told me she'd remember our time together fondly."

"That's what's most important," Bill added sagely.

Before Quinton could start up again, I said, "I should go check on everyone on the sales floor. See you guys later."

I zipped out of there, merely waving at Millicent the fire witch and Rex's brother Melvin. The cashiers were too busy handling customers anyway and I had work to do after stopping at Farley's place.

It was time to go camping and plant this damn thing in a proper place.

～

The drive to Farley's cottage, or should I say my former first home that I owned in town, was cathartic in a way. I'd left and returned to South Toms River many times at this point, but that cottage remained a place close to my heart.

When I turned off Double Trouble State Road onto the driveway up to my place, I couldn't help but smile. The flowers we had planted around the place to make the home nice and cozy for Farley still thrived. Maybe that old coot had decided to leave his cozy armchair once in a while to water the plants.

I snorted. Who was I kidding? It was probably Thorn's brother Will who had taken the time to mow the lawn and keep up with the other plants.

As I walked up to the door and knocked, I expected Thorn to answer the door, but to my surprise it was crusty old Farley. The former South Toms River pack leader didn't greet me warmly. He merely grunted and gestured for me to come inside.

"C'mon in, before you let out all the good air-conditioning." He limped back to his armchair.

A long time ago, back when Farley had to fight to maintain his place as pack leader, an old injury got him good and for some reason never wanted to heal. Pack healers alike couldn't get the stubborn injury to heal, and I wasn't surprised with a man like Farley.

"Where's Thorn?" I couldn't hear him in the house, only smell that he'd been here recently.

"He's in the back trying to sort through the camping supplies I stuffed into the shed."

Without thinking, I started gathering the empty cups Farley left on the end table next to the La-Z-Boy and snagging any wrappers littered on the floor.

"What're you doing, girl?" he snapped.

"Just helping out."

"We both know what you're doing." He eyed me up and down. "This is my place now and I'll take care of it. You and Will are always fussin' all the time."

I smiled. Instead of his usual gruffness, he sounded rather *pleasant*. And it was good to know Will was helping out around here.

"What's that Christmasy thing you got in your hand?" he asked.

"It's a Seed of the Fates." I explained what we needed to do with it.

"Why the hell are you carrying it around? For all you know, that thing could just pop up and eat you."

"Well, if it actually did sprout, I'd have a shot at surviving," I said. "Since I don't know how to make this thing grow, my only options are to carry it around until Thorn and I bury it nearby."

He took a sip of some bottled iced tea. "So that's why my boy is making a mess in the shed."

"Do you have some tents? I thought most of your stuff was burned in the fire." Back when I worked for the Daylight Dame and Mademoiselle Midnight at the ceramic mart, Farley's house caught on fire.

"We got plenty." He gestured for me to come closer. "You got some dragon seed fertilizer or something?"

"Fertilizer?"

"I mean shit, Natalya."

*Good God in heaven, that wasn't gonna happen*, I thought.

Farley must've missed my horrified face, for he added, "You should go see that weird ass dragon. The fat one?"

"You mean the *zmee*?"

"Yeah, you should see if that dragon got some fresh fertilizer."

I threw Farley a smile and bolted out the back door. "Sure, I'll think about it."

I was so done asking for *advice* from people. It would be a cold day in hell before you found me scooping up that three-headed dragon's excrement.

# CHAPTER NINETEEN

Not long after I'd left Farley's place, my phone jostled with a new message. Hopefully, Brenna had gotten back to me.

It was a message from Mom: *Come home tonight for a family meeting. Not optional. We need to make plans.*

I sighed, deciding I wouldn't go. The last thing I wanted to do was draw my family deeper into this fight.

My clever mother must've read my mind, for another message appeared not long after: *If you don't show up, you'll disappoint your* babushka.

Wow. I shook my head. She knew right where to hit me.

Another message arrived and I about chucked the phone out the window.

The message from Aggie read: *Your mom said you're back in town and there's a family meeting about the hellhounds. You better show up or I'm gonna kick your ass.*

Five additional messages showed up from cousins and my aunts and uncle. I put it on silent. I knew everyone meant well, but I didn't feel like dealing with them.

I just wanted that damn plant to sprout.

Was that too much to ask?

The day crept on while Thorn and I setup camp in Double Trouble State Park. When the time came for the meeting, it was Thorn who reminded me.

"You ready to go?"

"No."

I grabbed the flowerpot and we made our way back to the car. The trip to my parents' place didn't take long. Cars lined the whole street. Thorn and I had to park on the next block.

I expected to find my parents' Colonial quiet with folks waiting for me, but the house quaked from the roars of my uncles watching a survival show called *Naked & Afraid*. I'd seen an episode before and didn't understand why folks wanted to challenge themselves hunting and foraging while butt naked. Getting up was enough of a challenge.

I veered around my younger cousins who watched the TV in awe. Perhaps they hoped for something dramatic to happen, but these shows never revealed the good stuff.

I wasn't sure how this was supposed to be a serious meeting if everyone was groaning and yelling at the TV. As Thorn and I passed through the living room, three uncles watched some guy nurse his wounds. There were countless insect bites all over the contestants' legs and torsos.

One uncle cringed. "Who would do this for money? His little soldier will be itching for days."

I couldn't resist smiling as another uncle added, "Humans, I tell you. Fools."

Thorn and I finally made it into the kitchen where it was a standing only affair. Grandma, Mom, Aunt Vera, and Dad took up the seats at the kitchen table.

Mom motioned for me to come forward. "There she is."

My friends and family filled the room. I smiled at Aggie, Erica, and Karey. My friends from group therapy, Abby, Tyler, and Raj waved from the corner near the fridge while

Alex leaned against the counter and held Sveta. Even Thorn's brother Will, the Dawson family from the butchers, Jocelyn the manager at Kramkar's place, and Esmerelda from the brownie bakery came. Still no Brenna and she had yet to answer my text message. I was starting to worry that something was wrong with her.

Like any other family meeting, I spied bowls of dishes sprinkled here and there, along with a sizeable rack of lamb on the stove. Several empty plates on the table meant folks had helped themselves long before I arrived.

"You're late," Aunt Vera said.

"By twenty minutes," I replied.

"Don't worry," Grandma said. "They're just used to you always being on time." She chuckled a bit.

"Want me to make you a plate?" Erica offered.

"I'm not hungry." Everything smelled great, but I had far too much on my mind—even for food as amazing as Mom's.

"Make her a plate anyway to take home," Aunt Vera said to Erica. "Double the lamb portion. Will be good for her. She needs her strength."

Erica strode over to the stove and Aggie followed to help —or should I say help herself to another serving.

"Now that everyone is here," Dad said, "we can form a plan. We need a united front when those hellhounds return."

My hand rose. "There will be no united front," I said firmly. "We don't have the champion yet and those creatures are very dangerous. I will leave again if the heavy guns don't materialize."

Dad flashed me a sour look. "You're done running, daughter."

"Thorn and I have seen them firsthand," Aggie said carefully. "They're very dangerous; I will give you that." She tapped the counter to emphasize her point. "But they *aren't* immortal, and if they're solely focused on you, then as a pack, we can work together to kill them."

"How?" The word came out of my mouth and lacked any conviction.

"When you fought the hellhound in Central Park," Dad asked Aggie and Thorn, "did any of you get through its hide?"

"Barely," Thorn said. "The Yule Cat did get in a couple scratches on its face."

"Yule Cat?" Aunt Vera's face scrunched up in confusion.

I told them about my task from Seamus the leprechaun to collect used clothes from the Christmas Cat in Central Park. After we'd arrived, we'd encountered a shapeshifting creature that ate children during the holidays unless they wore new clothes. The poor Yule Cat was barely a match for the hellhound, which was much stronger, but less agile.

"The Christmas Cat sounds like a vile creature," Mom said.

"Since the cat harmed it, then we know the hellhounds have a vulnerability," Dad said. "We have a shot if we go for the head then. Maybe use arms if we must."

"We got a cannon then?" I asked drily. "There are five of them coming for me now and those things can become invisible at will. They can shrink and expand in size."

Alex appeared pensive. "Those aren't impossible odds though. Even with those abilities, they are still like *us*."

Will stepped forward. "If they're pack animals," he said between chews, "then we should be able to drive them into a trap."

Jocelyn nodded in agreement. "The trolls would be great at helping you steer them in the right direction. 'Cause even a ten-foot monster ain't gonna plow through a boulder weighing several tons."

The mood in the room lifted as more ideas spilled forth. Aunt Vera suggested drowning them in the nearby river, while Jocelyn threw out burying them so deep, they couldn't resurface. Raj even offered to teleport them to a shrine in the middle of nowhere in northern Asia. All these ideas sounded good. So why did I doubt them?

"Looks like we have many great ideas," Dad said. "But we must first separate them, and this must be done away from the human population. We don't need the warlocks sniffing around here when things go down."

I rather wished we had some spellcasters to offer a hand.

"There are many of us here. We should form teams," Tyler said, clearly eager to fight. "If the goal is the separate them, then engage, then the fastest runners can keep them busy."

"But they're after me," I interjected.

"So why did the hellhound chase the cat then?" Thorn's eyebrows rose. "They're hunters like Diana. They're like bloodhounds that *seek* weaker prey."

He had a good point there. "Tyler's idea might work then."

"Yes, yes." Dad nodded. "Do they follow an alpha?"

"Diana is their alpha," I explained, briefly feeling the collar she'd made me wear when I was captured.

"Will she come to fight too?" Aunt Vera asked.

No one else wanted to answer that question. Even Abby, who was more familiar with the world of mythical creatures, inclined her head.

"I hope not," I finally said.

# CHAPTER TWENTY

The July night was surprisingly warm, the air thick with the scent of pine and earth. The half-moon hung high in the sky and cast a silvery glow through the treetops. This particular spot in Jack Branch County Park was perfect for the magical seed. Thorn and I had run through here during the full moon countless times. Just touching the circle of trees around this glen brought back fond memories. Now all we had to do was wait.

Thorn and I sat on folding chairs, our fingers intertwined as we gazed at the small mound of dirt in front of us. We'd planted the seed by our tent four hours ago. So far nothing had happened. Even the ancient Celtic antiquities book in my lap had more action in it.

I sighed. "Do you think it's supposed to take this long?" I tried to read the entries on Celtic crosses, but my attention kept getting yanked away.

Thorn chuckled, his hand squeezing mine reassuringly. "Doesn't your mom say a watched pot doesn't boil? Patience is key here."

Easy for him to say. Thorn had always been the patient

one, the calm in my storm. While he could find solace in the gentle hum of nature, I couldn't shake the anticipation gnawing at me. I'd tried everything to distract myself—reading, napping, a partially filled-in Sudoku booklet—but nothing could divert my attention from that unyielding mound of earth.

A gentle breeze danced through the leaves, carrying the distant melodic trill of two whip-poor-wills. I shifted in my chair.

"You know," Thorn mused, breaking the silence, "I read somewhere that this would all be easier if we surrendered to the unknown."

"Surrender to the unknown, huh?" I gave him the side-eye.

"It's a valuable lesson in patience."

"Forewarned is forearmed." I abandoned the book to take in the sky. "And have you mastered the art of surrender?"

He chuckled again. "Maybe not entirely, but I'm learning."

We fell into a comfortable silence, but what happened back at the cranberry farm flicked at me until I said, "Hey, Thorn. Care to talk about how you lied to Ernest about killing Calliope?"

"I didn't lie." My mate didn't so much as flinch.

"How? Did you use old magic?"

He shook his head. "At the time, all I could think about was you and your family. You looked like your usual calm self on the outside, but I knew you were cornered. I did what I had to do." He turned to face me and I couldn't look away. "I love you more than anything."

We stared at each other for a bit, and I considered all the times I'd been willing to shift the heavens for Thorn.

"What about Calliope?" I whispered.

"Killing her would've been very wrong, but I had no choice. I was hoping the fairies' plan kicked in before I had to do it." His chest rose and fell in a long sigh. "Would you believe your dad kept blinking at me to *not* do it?"

"Good luck facing my family after pulling something like that."

He shuddered. "I'm not sure what's worst. Shaming yourself or winning Trivial Pursuit against the Stravinskys."

I laughed. The feeling felt good. Practically normal.

"You know," he began, his voice soft, "after all this settles down, what do you say we plan something special for the fall? Something to look forward to?"

My gaze flicked to the dirt pile. "I can't think of anything fun right now. I just want things to be quiet for a while."

He nodded. "We don't have to go far. Maybe a cozy cabin in the woods away from the chaos. Or we could go to a quiet bed and breakfast somewhere."

I shook my head. "I appreciate the thought, but I'm done traveling. I just want to be normal. Whatever that is. No more fearing for our lives or our family's." My voice rose. "I want that damn seed to grow and end this shit."

Thorn got up and pulled me into a tight embrace. I sagged against him, trying to relax, but unable to. A single tear traced a path down my cheek.

"We'll get through this, babe," he whispered. "And when it's over, we'll have our peace."

An hour later, we settled down for the night and left the flap open to let in the gentle breeze. I couldn't tear my eyes away from the pile of dirt, watching it as if my gaze alone could coax the seed to sprout.

As the night wore on, I stared out into the darkness, contemplating the uncertain future. Before sleep claimed me, I could've sworn I felt a subtle change in the air, a whisper of magic. Or perhaps it was wishful thinking, a desperate hope that the seed would grow. With that thought lingering in my mind, I closed my eyes to rest for the challenges ahead.

～

Not long after eight in the morning, my phone rang. I shuffled in the tangle of sleeping bags until I found my phone. Thorn's eyes opened, but he didn't move.

"Hello?" I said.

"Nat, I got some news," Karey began to say.

At the sound of my sister-in-law's voice, Thorn's head rose.

Karey continued. "The trees near the cabins in Maine finally reached out to me. There was a great fight when the hellhounds came sniffing around."

I nearly dropped the phone. "Uncle Boris…"

"I don't know what happened to him. Only that many trees burned, and it took some time for the news to be passed along." Her voice sounded detached. "The hellhounds have been heading south for a while now. I'm guessing they could be three hours away. Maybe less. Prepare yourself, sister. I'm gonna call Mom and Dad so they can get everyone in position."

A headache formed on the back of my head, and I squeezed my eyes shut to work through the pain. The grim reaper was closing in.

And the seed had yet to sprout.

I got up.

"Anything happen?" Thorn asked.

"Nope."

Thorn cursed. "I don't like this. We should go. Now."

"She said we had at *least* three hours."

"Three hours or *less*, Natalya."

The pain deepened, spreading until I cringed as if hit. "I know. I know. I want to try one more thing. One more." I slipped on my shoes. If I stopped moving, I wouldn't move anymore. The pain retreated when I grabbed my keys.

"Get up," I told Thorn as I dug up the seed and tossed it back in the flowerpot. "I need to check on an idea from Farley."

Thorn's eyes formed slits. "Where we are we going?"

"To get some fertilizer."

# CHAPTER TWENTY-ONE

With the clock ticking far too loudly, Thorn and I jumped in the car to go see the *zmee*. Briefly, I stopped at a gas station for garbage bags and some antiseptic spray. If I was gonna be collecting dragon feces, I wouldn't be touching it. Period.

The last visit to the three-headed dragon to learn the whereabouts of the Basilisk King had gone awry, but this time I planned to get in there and get back out quickly.

It didn't take us long to race about five miles south of town to Jake Branch Park. From there, I spotted a familiar path next to a snowplow shed. We hurried through the woods until the path ended at a toolshed surround by haphazard piles of scrap metal, televisions, and other bits of decades-old junk. Not a single pile of shit to be seen.

I didn't bother trying to sneak in. The *zmee* probably heard us approaching from a mile away. We strolled out of the sun and up to the shed, sidestepping a bicycle with no wheels and a pile of car stereos. Everything stank from exposure, but at least we were cooler once we stood under the shade of an oak tree jutting out of the back the shed.

"Hey, *Zmee*. I'm back again," I shouted in Russian.

That dirty dragon shifted inside the house and I caught the sounds of bits and baubles tumbling about.

"We need to talk," I added in English.

"We've talked enough," one of the dragon's heads grunted.

"And I'm not gonna fall for any tricks," a different voice added. Likely another head. "There's nothing we want."

Thorn folded his arms, clearly annoyed.

I had a feeling the *zmee* would pull this. "I honestly need help. Nothing underhanded."

I hefted the pot in one hand and stirred the dirt with the other until the seed surfaced. "I need to summon a champion —a dragon. Do you know about a Seed of the Fates and would your…droppings help it grow?"

Something inside the house jostled. The door handle rattled before a voice—the third one—said, "Don't you open that door! She's marked by a goddess."

The second one moaned, "But she has a seed from the Fates! The Fates!" It squealed with delight. "Those are rare. And so beautiful. They have so much potential."

"You're an idiot," the first voice said. "Her pursuers would rip our house, and us, apart."

Seeing an opportunity I said, "If you can help me in any way, I'll leave peacefully. I promise."

The door opened inward with a yawn. A scaly hand with a four-fingered claw appeared. The *zmee* wiggled and jerked with its tiny arms and legs and pulled its body out. After a bit of time, the three heads emerged. Its rear end remained inside.

"Can you see it now?" the first head snapped at the second. "It's just a seed."

The second head stretched until it loomed above me. Its amber eyes glowed with adoration. "Where did you get it?"

I told them how I'd bartered with the dryad at The Gray

Glen for the prize. "Now, I'm trying to get it to grow. Do you know anything about it?"

"What makes you think we know about it?" the first head asked.

The third head laughed. "Guess we missed that info at the last international dragon meeting."

I sighed. "Fellas, I'm serious."

The second head lowered until we faced each other. This was the closest I'd ever gotten to them. Thorn edged toward us, ready to pounce if the *zmee* made trouble. The dragon exhaled and I expected its breath to be rotten, but it was sickeningly sweet.

"So beautiful," it murmured. "Have you been keeping it warm?"

"Warm?" I glanced down at the pot. "It's a seed, not an egg."

All three heads busted out laughing and my mouth dropped open. Was it serious? Good God, was my uncle right this whole time? Boris suggested setting the seed on fire right after I'd gotten it.

"You shouldn't have told her," the first head said.

"Do you see the look on her face?" the third added. "Get the camera!"

"I'm too tired to scoot back inside," the first head replied. "Go get it yourself."

I picked up the seed and found it quite cold—even with the humidity out here. "Do I still need to plant it?"

"Probably," the second head said. "If you leave it here with me, I can protect it."

I leaned away from the head to get out of striking distance. "No need."

Thorn grabbed the back of my shirt and tugged. I followed him to keep backing away, even when the second head added, "Sure you won't come inside for supper?"

"I've learned enough, thank you," I replied.

"You idiot," the third head said. "You don't ask your prey to just *come* inside."

The second head nipped at the first. "It might've worked. You're always mocking me."

"I'd stop making fun of you, if you'd stop saying stupid shit."

The argument continued as Thorn and I walked away. A new plan formed in my mind: Time to bring the fire. A lot of it.

~

The morning shift had already started by the time Thorn and I pulled up to The Bends' parking lot. He dropped me off so I could run inside. The scent of fried food wafted through the air—probably from Kramkar's business to entice customers from Bill's place.

As I approached the entrance, my phone buzzed in my pocket, startling me. I pulled it out to find Erica's name flashing on the screen. I groaned and quickly answered with, "Hey, Erica, now's not a good time."

"I'm so sorry about this, Nat." Erica sounded breathless. "Thank goodness you picked up. I need some help at The Bends."

At least I was right outside. "What's up?"

Erica must've been in the back office. I couldn't hear much from the main floor. "Mrs. Kite is causing a ruckus again, and this time it's worse. She brought her *whole* damn family, and they're demanding compensation for a broken handle on an early 20th century gramophone. She said it was broken beforehand and Bill made a written promise guaranteeing quality or a refund."

I smacked my lips. That harpy was so damn good at

making a scene. "I'll be there in a sec. Hey, is Millicent working now?"

"Yeah, do you need to speak to her?"

"I'll talk to her once I'm inside," I replied before ending the call.

I quickened my pace and entered the building through the front this time. Dodging curious stares, I made my way to the counter where Erica was dealing with a harpy commotion. You couldn't miss them—the whole place stank like the cheap vanilla perfume Mrs. Kite wore. The conniving creature came in dressed in her usual bedazzled jeans and jean jacket and screeched at the poor clerk. She waved some kind of letter about.

"Are you going to help me or what?" Mrs. Kite snapped. "Or do you need to make another phone call?"

"I'll be happy to help you," Erica replied, "but I need you to stop harassing my staff."

Four other harpies, all of them covered in shiny, over-the-top glamours blustered and complained to anyone who'd listen.

"Can you believe the kind of service my sister is getting?" said one busty harpy dressed in a construction-worker orange velour jogger set.

Another nodded in a jailbird black and white stripped romper, clearly disgusted with a frown filling her whole face.

"Dirty thieves." The third gestured wildly to make sure *everyone* noticed. "All of 'em."

I approached discreetly and examined the antique record player in question on the checkout counter. The broken handle confirmed Mrs. Kite's claim, but something felt off. I returned to the back office and jumped on a nearby workstation. Since my login still worked, I scrolled through the old receipts, finally finding the one associated with the record player.

After printing off the evidence, I rejoined Erica and Mrs. Kite. The moment that harpy spotted me, I could've sworn her black feathers rustled with disgust under her glamour.

"You," she spat. "I heard you don't work here anymore. You have no say here, Nat."

"Guess I returned just in time." I slammed the receipt on the counter. I didn't have time for this bullshit. "This is the original description, and it doesn't mention a broken handle. Based on that, you're not entitled to compensation. Yet. Again."

Erica stepped forward. "Nat speaks for the store. Stop making a scene and leave, please."

Mrs. Kite huffed but eventually left with her disgruntled family in tow. I breathed a sigh of relief, realizing I had to get back to my original mission.

Turning to Erica, I shook my head. "Bill needs to ban her for life."

Erica smiled. "If he didn't make so much money from her, he would. Didn't you need to speak to Millicent?"

"Yeah." I glanced around and spotted the fire witch at the far-end register. You couldn't miss her since she was the only person with bright purple hair in the store.

"I'll cover for her while you chat," Erica offered.

We walked over and I tapped Millicent on the shoulder.

"Hey, there, I need your help with something," I said. "Can we talk for a sec?"

Millicent looked intrigued. "Sure, Nat. What's going on?"

"Let's chat in private." I gestured to the back office doors.

Erica took Millicent's place while we found a quieter spot to chat in the back office. Only Quinton worked in there, but when he spotted us, he waved and returned to the sales floor.

"I'm not sure how to say this, but I need your fire magic. Can you create flames as hot as a dragon's?"

Millicent raised an eyebrow. "I'm not sure. How hot is a dragon's fire?"

I shrugged. "Not sure, but I need enough heat to torch a magical seed."

Millicent grinned. "If all I need to do is set something on fire, count me in."

I sagged against the fire witch and hugged her for the first time in my life. "Oh, thank you."

I shot a quick text to Erica explaining the situation while the fire witch laughed a bit. "This must be serious," she said. "Where are we going?"

"It's not far, I promise."

We hurried out of the back office to the dock. The bright summer sun briefly blinded me. When the sun retreated, the oak trees behind the market shuddered and distant heavy thuds grew stronger. And closer.

Then the forest grew quiet.

"What was that?" Millicent asked.

"Oh shit," I breathed.

My time had run out.

# CHAPTER TWENTY-TWO

The fire witch bolted down the path around The Bends toward the parking lot. A single, middle-aged man waltzed in and stared at her in confusion. I zipped past him and caught up with her. As she darted around a motorcycle and glanced over her shoulder, I waved my arms for her to keep running.

"You don't wanna see what's coming!" I yelled.

The SUV's tires screeched as Thorn swerved around the parking lot. He pulled up next to us and we jumped in.

"What were you *doing* in there?" Thorn asked. "I almost ran in."

*Was he serious?* "We were planning a Pampered Chef party."

Thorn avoided the Garden State Parkway, or the Parkway as we called it, and hit the side streets to take us southward back to the state park. "I alerted the pack before all hell broke loose. Everyone's heading to Jake Branch to help draw the hellhounds away from us."

We reached Double Trouble State Road and raced southeast. All we had to do was reach the park entrance and we'd be far enough from people to unleash the dragon. Having enough time to *summon* the dragon was another matter.

The park entrance loomed ahead and my hope lifted. Thankfully, the Sunday morning traffic was non-existent, and no one spotted the twenty-foot-tall hounds barreling our way.

Thorn slowed down to make the turn. As we turned, the back of the SUV lifted and lurched hard to the right.

"Fuck!" Thorn's arm shot out to brace me. In the backseat, Millicent screamed. The SUV slammed into the tree line and fell onto its side.

I didn't wait for the hellhounds to pluck me out like a tasty sardine from a tin can. I unbuckled my seatbelt and scrambled into the back.

"I'll get her," Thorn shouted. "Run for the woods."

Briefly our gazes connected, and endearments jumped between us. I escaped out of a broken window, cutting my palms in the process. I had little time to think about the pain as I ran away from the open parking lot toward the thicker clusters of trees. With each step, the wolf within whined for me to run faster. To surrender to my natural form to hide.

The ground continued to murmur as the hellhounds closed in. Bushes appeared too sparse, the nearby trees too spread out to hide behind. The interior of Jack Branch County Park began to coalesce. The places the pack had run through like the hiking trails to the observation deck, fell away from my mind. I tried to grasp for a place to hide, but I couldn't think of anything.

*Think, think.*

After too many seconds of indecision, I ran south. The gentle gurgles from the creek tugged me forward. When I crossed Jack Branch Creek to veer southward, the trees behind me parted like curtains announcing the stage's main attraction. A hellhound with piercing light-gray eyes barreled in my direction. I stood in the knee-deep water and stared at it like a fool. Before I could virtually shock myself back into reality, the gray-eyed hellhound in front of me opened its mouth. Every single sharp tooth grew within my field of vision. My heartbeat hammered against my ribs. The sounds around me ceased. All that was left was my end approaching.

Out of nowhere, Thorn crossed my path to head east while Millicent ran south. The gray-eyed hellhound darted after him, but the four others wouldn't be deterred by such shiny distractions. Two of them closed in. The smaller one between the pair, a runt with burnt-orange jowls, surged forward to sink its teeth into my right leg. It yanked me back hard enough for my hip to pop out of the socket. *Ouch.* I screamed in mid-air before a larger hellhound with one ear bit into my shoulder. Horrific pain streaked down my torso as each tried to pull me in a different direction.

*Fight, Natalya, Fight.*

All I could see was white-hot pain. Breathtaking pain. Not far from me, a monstrous snaggle-toothed hellhound corned Millicent. I had to do something. Anything.

I opened my mouth to speak, but the One-Earred hellhound growled and bit down harder. Darkness seeped into the edge of my vision. The other hellhounds scrambled to retrieve the prize, namely me, when I finally sucked in a breath to scream out a spell.

A heartbeat later, a screeching wind picked up the hellhounds. The whirlwind snapped the branches off the trees and flung brush high into the air. The Runt and One-Ear released me as they flailed. The ankle holster with my goblin blade was tossed into the trees.

I landed hard onto the back of the fifth hellhound. As the pink-nosed hound turned around, I flopped off its back and landed on my face in the tall grass.

Pink Nose yipped with glee and stomped on my back to pin me down. I growled and scratched at the dirt to free myself. With each moment that passed, I couldn't suck in a full breath.

Somehow, I managed to turn my head to see a great white light fill the forest. The light forced me to squeeze my eyes shut. Suddenly, the dirt in my face receded. The weight off my back lifted. Warm arms wrapped around me. I craned my head to see Thorn. Behind him, a white wizard wearing a long, black coat thrust a majestic ebony staff into the ground. Sparks danced across the sky before another lightning bolt forced the hellhounds to retreat a bit.

Nick Fenton had arrived, and as usual, he'd made quite the entrance. Thank goodness.

The white wizard, along with Brenna and Millicent, ran to us. Once Nick touched Thorn's arm, we were whisked away in another flash of light.

We teleported to an open field on the southern edge of Jack Branch County Park. I recognized a nearby hiking trail. Poor Millicent collapsed while Thorn managed to hold me. Blood from a grisly wound on his ribs trickled down his leg.

"Are you alright?" Thorn asked me.

I almost laughed and groaned instead.

"Don't answer that," he added.

Brenna wrapped her arms around the fire witch and helped her stand.

Nick placed his hand on my shoulder. Two palm-sized bitemarks marred my skin. "What did they do to you?"

"How bad is it?" Thorn craned his head to peek at my injuries.

"Good to see you too, Fenton," I managed to say.

"You think this is *good*?" The white wizard snorted. "You and I should aim for much quieter reunions."

I couldn't resist laughing. Every deep breath hurt like hell.

"She's a wreck. Let's tackle the dislocation first," Nick said. "I need her to lie flat so I can do a reduction."

"What's that?" Thorn asked as he put me down.

Millicent was sitting up now, so Brenna came over to assist. "He needs to manipulate the dislocated hip joint to guide the femoral head back into the hip socket."

"Doesn't it just *pop* back in on its own?" Thorn asked.

Brenna refused to look up as she said, "That won't happen if the socket is crushed. He has to repair that too."

My mate's mouth formed an "oh."

Nick worked quickly to place his hands on my hip first. "I can't make this feel nice, Nat."

"Just take care of it," I grunted.

"Knock her out," Thorn growled to Nick.

"No, the hellhounds are coming—" I bit out.

Thorn's head snapped in Nick's direction. "Lights. Out."

I blinked and then everyone around me except Nick was standing again. Damn it, that sneaky wizard knocked me out. I eyed the wizard with contempt as Thorn spoke with my dad on the phone. The pack was in position. Millicent must've fished the seed from my pocket. Brenna and the fire witch stooped before a dark patch of earth.

"Aren't you supposed to do what the patient asks?" It was much easier to speak this time. "How much time did I lose?"

"Five minutes." The annoyed expression on Nick's face told me he'd wanted a lot longer to work. "You tried to wake up too many times."

I lifted my head and listened. No sign of the hellhounds yet. I also noticed I was missing something *important*.

"My goblin blade—" I said.

"I found it trying to crawl back to you," Nick said with a single raised eyebrow. "Would you like it back?"

I shook my head. "The holster is broken. Just keep it safe until I need it again."

He nodded.

"Can I get up now?" I asked. All my fingers and toes wiggled. That had to be a good sign, right?

"Do I need to put you to sleep again?"

Before he could knock me out, I rose on unsteady feet. My shoulder was almost healed, but my hip felt like rolling about in shards of glass. Thorn finished his call and joined us.

"How long will it take to summon your dragon?" Nick asked, tension evident in his voice.

"Hopefully not long." I hobbled over to Brenna and Millicent. Thorn tried to help me, but I shook my head. I didn't want to be carried anymore.

Thorn turned to Nick and said, "How did you know where we were?"

"Aggie's kept us up to date," Brenna said as she placed her hand on the seed. "It's gonna take an inferno to make this grow. It's gobbling up the heat in this spot already."

Nick grasped my shoulder and gently tugged me to sit. "If you're going to be a stubborn patient, at least let me heal you while you work."

His healing magic flooded my system again.

Millicent's gaze was trained on the seed as she cast a simple warming spell, but the earth remained unyielding. The scent of burnt cinnamon spread across the field. The air grew humid and the temperature rose, but nothing happened.

"You're gonna need a maple one," Brenna said. "That thing's a thermal absorber."

Millicent swapped out her oak wand for a maple one as Brenna instructed.

Thorn shifted nervously. "We don't have a lot of time," he warned.

"We need more heat," Brenna said.

"Can you help?" Thorn asked Brenna.

She ran her hand through her dark, chin-length hair and bit her lower lip. "This isn't your standard growth magic here."

"We don't have time for this." My insides screamed for me to sit. Every movement hurt, but I scrambled closer.

"I'm not done." Nick followed me, clearly annoyed.

I didn't care. I was only ten feet away when I spied a tiny green bud had sprouted on the seed.

"Let's cook this little fella." Millicent fished a cigarette out of her bag. She placed the unlit cig between her lips and closed her eyes. Dark red and burnt orange lights flickered around her, the air crackling with energy. The grass around the seed withered, the rocks darkened, and the wind picked up.

Six more buds formed and expanded into a head, four limbs, and a tail. The dragon was taking shape, writhing and stretching out its tiny vine-like limbs. But the fire witch's flames were dying. Millicent clenched her teeth until she bit off the end of the cigarette.

"She needs help," I murmured to Nick.

"I'm barely holding you up." He reached into his black coat with his free hand and withdrew an elm wand from one of his magical pockets. "I can help a little." He pointed the stalk toward the pile and scorching flames fed the writhing dragon.

But it still wasn't enough.

The pain in my hip returned like a tsunami threatening to

pull me under. My knees weakened. Nick's healing attention had wavered.

Thorn stepped in to hold me up. "Got you."

"No, I need to help," I breathed.

"You're not using old magic," Thorn warned.

"We have no choice." I whispered the fire spell Tamara had taught me. Instead of picturing that piece of toast back in Tamara's kitchen, I imagined a great bonfire. All it needed was gasoline.

"Nat, you're too weak," Nick warned. "Not now."

It took a moment, but the magic swelled inside me, and fire flowed from my hands to the growing dragon. The pain in my hip magnified twenty times, but I gritted my teeth and channeled my agony toward the task at hand.

Nick's hand shot from my shoulder to my hip. "You're ripping apart what I'm weaving back together."

The dragon's body unfolded like a living tapestry. Its scales, resembling delicate ivy leaves, unfurled and caught the sunlight, creating a dazzling display of emerald hues. As the creature continued to grow, its limbs extended outward, transforming into sinuous vines. The twirling branches thickened, forming strong, knotty rootlike limbs that anchored the majestic beast to the earth. Progress was finally made, and the dragon grew until it stood at the height of the surrounding trees. The creature roared, its eyes fixed on me.

A wide-eyed Thorn growled, ready to defend, while Millicent crawled back as fast as she could.

I knew I should flee, but somehow, I was rooted to where I stood. Something inside me told me to stand my ground. To accept my fate.

Instead of attacking me, the dragon approached, bowed its head, and closed its eyes. The once-shiny green bud had transformed into a magnificent, scaled creature. Its eyes reflected intelligence and determination.

Thorn blinked in disbelief, and Millicent slowly raised her head. "I... I didn't think it would work."

"Beautiful," Brenna said.

I reached out to touch the dragon's snout. The surface appeared as delicate as newborn leaf, yet as unyielding as stone. "Time to kick some ass."

We didn't have long to celebrate.

The dragon's head snapped to the north, and it screeched in that direction.

"Looks like we got company coming," Nick said wistfully.

"Let's go!" I searched around for the fire witch, but she was already making a run for it toward the east. A part of me wished I could join her. "Will she be all right?"

"I told her to find Double Trouble State Road and run home," Thorn said.

It was for the best. I owed her big time.

The dragon stretched out its wings and took to the skies.

We sprinted south as the hellhounds' barks echoed through the trees. A quarter of a mile into the woods, they finally caught up with us.

Nick opened fire first. He retrieved his white staff and briefly turned to engage. White hot lightning crackled from the tip and arched toward the beasts, lighting up the forest floor around us. Brenna wasn't far behind, throwing fallen trees into the hellhounds' path. Thorn and I kept running.

Above us, the dragon kept pace with us, its majestic wings slicing through the air.

My gut stabbed at me again and I stumbled but didn't fall.

As we raced toward our waiting pack, Thorn shouted over the din of pursuit, "Almost there! The first team is ready, people!"

Breathless and aching, I nodded, the urgency in my veins pushing me to press on. The clearing where the first team waited loomed ahead.

Suddenly, a colossal form stormed through the trees. One-Ear advanced on us. Nick slowed down and raised his staff in the air. The light behind me brightened as the air grew hazy. Brenna jumped in to assist and commanded the roots of the trees to entangle the beast in front. Yet, their efforts only slowed it briefly.

Emerging into the clearing, I spotted the first team waiting. My pack members, more than twenty of them, circled and howled. Their eagerness peppered the air. We reached the middle of the field as One-Ear closed in. Its shadow grew larger behind me. Bit by bit.

Before the hellhound swooped in, the dragon descended from above to intercept. Its massive jaws opened, and it clamped down on One-Ear's neck, sending them crashing into the foliage.

The werewolves howled and yipped with glee, luring Pink Nose and Light Gray Eyes away from me. The pack sprinted off to the east with the two in pursuit. Now only the Runt and Snaggletooth remained on my tail.

Thorn caught up with me and nudged me southward. My vision grew blurry. We ran side by side and I used his pace to keep me going through the hip pain and exhaustion. We reached the tree line and slipped back into the forest. The ground rumbled as if something even larger approached us, but from underground instead of aboveground.

Were more reinforcements coming?

Snaggletooth nipped at Runt to urge it to run faster. They crushed the underbrush to draw closer. The smaller hellhound dared to snap at me and I pivoted on my heel. I shouldn't have turned around—even for a half-second. The Runt opened its mouth, its foul breath hot against my face. If it bit me again, I might not get up.

I had to believe in the *impossible*.

In that split second, I pictured the red apple with the green kiss imprint from Grandma. I extended my hand and let my imagination run wild. The Runt's crimson teeth darkened as the fangs transformed into ice shards. The beast howled in pain and rubbed its face on the ground. Mounds in the earth rose out of the ground around the animal, forming a hole. Thank goodness Kramkar and the other trolls came to intervene. Heavy boulders rose on the sides and fell in to pin the beast. The rocks jostled and jumped, but the now-toothless runt shook itself free, jumped out of the house, and took after me again.

Meanwhile, Thorn and Nick tried to draw Snaggletooth after them. With a twist of its great head, the beast plowed into Thorn and sent him sprawling into the trees. Nick teleported away just in time.

"Thorn!" I almost ran to him, but once the Runt breathing down my neck came for me, I bolted to the south again.

"Nat, c'mon!" Brenna was up ahead trying to clear a path.

Snaggletooth ignored Nick's waving arms and joined the Runt. Racing southward with Brenna at my side, we plunged through the thick woods. My injured hip grew numb, but determination fueled my every step.

Another clearing appeared beside an access road with two cars waiting—my aunt Vera's minivan and another with Alex waiting behind the wheel. Gasping, I leaped into the minivan as Brenna joined Alex in the other vehicle.

Aunt Vera slammed her foot on the accelerator, and we peeled down the street. Us to the east and Alex to the west.

"Thank you," I breathed.

Aunt Vera's grip tightened on the steering wheel as the van shook and hit fifty miles per hour. The roads dipped and curved, forcing her to slow down.

As the wind rushed through the open window, I sagged against the seat. I wouldn't have long to rest, but I'd take it while I could. Before I could close my eyes, Nick materialized in the backseat with Brenna.

"Holy shit," the earth witch said. "Those things are vicious."

"They're no smarter than pups," my aunt bit out. "Stay sharp, my friends."

Nick reached around the passenger seat and touched my shoulder. The searing pain in my hip eased. "How you holding up?"

"Is Brenna okay?" My voice sounded way too winded.

"I didn't mean her," he said with amusement. "I meant you."

"I'm okay, Natalya," Brenna said. "Just worry about yourself."

The ground shook as the trees behind us fell over. Snaggletooth and the Runt came running after us.

"Damn it," I groaned. "Guess, they didn't go after the second car."

The hellhounds couldn't keep up with the minivan, but they sprinted after us nonetheless.

"We can outrun them," Aunt Vera said. She even cackled as she hit a sharp corner and turned with a NASCAR driver's finesse.

The Runt took a great leap, and nearly landed on top of the car. Aunt Vera swerved out of the way, and almost clipped a tree.

"*Moduk!*" she yelled. "You idiots can't outmaneuver me."

Suddenly, Pink Nose and Light Gray Eyes showed up on the road ahead of us. Aunt Vera slammed on the brakes, but it was too late. Light Gray Eyes rammed the front of the car and sent us flying. The world outside my window became a whirlwind as the van flipped. Time slowed to a surreal crawl, each rotation dragging me through a disorienting void of sound. Colors blurred into streaks, and the once familiar forest became an abstract painting of impending disaster. In that moment, I was lost in the ethereal space between the van's vomit-inducing somersaults.

We were left upside down next to the trees.

Thanks to my seatbelt, the only marbles that were tossed about were the ones in my head. I turned around, hoping that Nick and Brenna had teleported away, but the white wizard, now hanging upside down, stared back at me with a growing frown.

"I've had enough of this," he growled.

"Is everyone OK?" Brenna asked.

I checked on my aunt. She was fumbling with her seatbelt.

"The damn thing is broken." She ripped the seatbelt off and crawled out of the rolled-down window.

Heavy thuds approached from all sides.

"We can't stay in here," Brenna said.

I unclipped my seatbelt and shifted to break the passenger-side window when I spotted Pink Nose barreling in my direction. I scrambled to get out of the car through the driver's side window instead.

I expected to find the three hellhounds waiting for me, but they were heading to the spellcasters. All the while, Brenna and Nick were arguing.

"Don't do it!" she yelled at him. "You're too weak to wield the warp wand."

The spellcasters had already exited the vehicle and were about to facedown the hellhounds farther down the road. Nick reached into his coat and withdrew a crimson wand. I'd never seen one of those before. Spellcasters usually used weapons made from elements like wood. Nick's weapon was shiny and had tiny, glittering diamond-like stones along the shaft.

What the hell was a warp wand?

Brenna tried to snatch it away from him, but Nick teleported to the other side of the road.

Before I could run to them, the dragon appeared over the tree line and slammed into Snaggletooth. My champion had taken far too many hits. Its tail was gone, and bits of its ivy leaf scales had been ripped off to reveal vulnerable muted green skin underneath.

The pair snapped and hissed as their mouths and claws tried to grasp a vulnerable point on the other. The agile dragon got the upper hand and wrapped its long neck around the hellhound. With a sharp jerk, the dragon flipped the hellhound over, then sank its thorny teeth into the hellhound's mouth. The dragon screeched as it ripped the hound's tooth out. The hellhound roared and bit back, ripping one of the dragon's wings off. A leg was clipped off next. A lost wing didn't slow my champion down. With a mighty roar, the dragon spewed a stream of ice. The arch hit the trees and froze everything it hit, including Snaggletooth.

My beautiful dragon was left crawling away from Snaggletooth's frozen body. The dragon tried to lift its head and failed.

It was dying.

"No!" My cry was swallowed away as I turned in horror to see Light Gray Eyes and the Runt storming toward Nick. That damn wizard sat down by the road and held the warp wand in the air. A crimson glow grew around him and the ground shook.

"I'm here!" I yelled and ran to intercept. "It's me you've come for!"

But the hellhounds ignored me, seemingly drawn to the strange lights. The wind shifted and I caught a new scent. Nick smelled like me now.

With One Ear and Snaggletooth down for the count, only three hellhounds remained, and they raced toward Nick. He'd saved me far too many times in the past and yet again today. This had to end now before someone else I cared about died.

I had to be the *heroine* of this story.

I ran harder and pushed myself to leap through the air. With a kick of wind via old magic, I was propelled into the path to intercept. I rolled to stand between the hounds and Nick.

I stretched my arms out. Let them come for me. Those bastards wouldn't miss this target. Pink Nose reached me first. It grasped my left arm and shoulder, nearly swallowing my head. The pain was immediate, but now that I'd had them close, I could act. Light Gray Eyes scrambled to grab too. I wanted them to touch me. Fight over me. They had to be close for this final act.

As Light Gray Eyes bit my right arm, I recalled the day in Tamara's parlor when she'd taught me earth magic. The lessons came fast—including one on the fundamental exchange in magic. Tamara had shown me, through quite the cruel demonstration, that the power I needed could be drawn from within or from *another* party.

*"Take back what I stole from you,"* that horrible woman had demanded.

Those words circled my head on repeat. I could see Tamara's boastful sneer and instead of feeling fearful, a calm settled over me. I'd take back the freedom Diana and her hellhounds had stolen from me. I spoke the words to draw power. In an instant, the lifeforce of Light Gray Eye and the Runt flooded my body. The sugary-sweet feeling was short-lived as Pink Nose abandoned pursuing Nick to aid its fallen comrades. It bit deep into my back to rip me off.

The moment its teeth penetrated my skin, I reached for it too. There was glorious strength there. An eternal fountain of youth waiting to be sipped. And I greedily drank. Even after Pink Nose let go, I sunk my claws into its flesh and refused to release it.

Before I blacked out from my wounds, I fell to the ground next to three dried-out husks.

Diana's hellhounds were no more.

# CHAPTER TWENTY-FOUR

Waking up wrapped in your grandmother's quilts was everything—especially when you realized you'd cheated death again. I was facing the wall in my parents' spare bedroom and the sun hadn't risen yet. I tried to turn over to draw the comforting scent of my mother closer when a familiar voice said, "Go back to sleep, Natalya."

Nick must've pushed a sleep spell on me, for I immediately grew drowsy. At least, the pain was gone.

"Not yet," I whispered. "What day is it?"

"Wednesday."

So I'd slept for four days straight. I licked my dry lips. "We haven't chatted in a while."

"We can talk later." The wizard sat on a seat next to the bed. He'd draped his black coat over the chair and wore nothing more a black T-shirt and jeans. Not a single piece of lint or dirt marred his clothes, but I wasn't surprised. Nick had far more stringent cleanliness habits than me.

"How's your work at the medical clinic going?" My voice was slurred.

"I'm not falling for it. Sleep."

"Still a killjoy." I managed to turn over, but it took me a while.

Nick grinned at me, and I realized I'd missed my friend. My best friend.

"Why do I feel numb all over?" I asked.

"You're quite the light sleeper so I gave you a little something to help you heal."

I rolled my eyes. "At least you didn't strap me down."

"I was tempted."

Now that I could see him clearly—even in the dim room —he appeared tired with a furrowed brow and wrinkles at the corners of his eyes. He even sagged on the seat.

My eyelids drooped, but I fought to keep them open. "You didn't answer my question."

He rubbed at the dark stubble on his chin. "I'm still at the clinic and I'm thriving."

"I assumed you were busy, so I've kept quiet. Why haven't I heard from you?" I asked carefully. "Did Brenna ask you to help me?"

Nick glanced at me, then his gaze shifted to his hands resting on his thighs. "Brenna didn't ask me to come. After she told me about the hellhounds, I decided to help."

"Why?" I tried to sit up a bit and failed. "I would've been fine on my own."

He gave me a familiar look of disbelief. "You're more than capable, but should I list how many times I've shown up to find you this close to dying?" Nick demonstrated how close with the narrow space between his fingers.

I personally would've added a couple handspans in there.

Nick continued. "Dr. Frank told me I needed to focus on myself—hence why you haven't heard from me." He laughed a little. "He told me I needed to save myself before I saved someone else—"

I lost consciousness for a moment, but I snapped awake again. "True."

We sat in silence for a spell as the faint glow from the rising sun touched the corners of the room. The only sound was the gentle ticks from an ancient alarm clock my parents refused to throw away. The darn thing never kept the correct time.

"If I asked you to come around more often, would you?" I whispered.

"That goes both ways." His head tilted in a questioning manner. "Are you gonna come to group therapy more often?"

"Dr. Frank told me he'd hunt me down. So yes, you'll see me more often."

He nodded, pleased with my words. "I have something for you. Give me your hand," he said.

"Are you trying to change the subject again?" I mumbled.

He shook his head as his relaxed expression fell away. "No."

I dragged my numb hand from under the blankets and flipped it over to reveal my palm. "Wanna exchange germs like old times?"

Nick leaned forward and placed something cold in the middle of palm. All I had to do was feel the object's lightness and my broken heart flopped to the floor. I sucked in a breath as my chest tightened.

"The seed." A warm tear streaked down my cheek. "I was hoping…"

"Not long after you defeated the hellhounds, he tried to reach you again, but he never made it."

"So it was a boy?"

He gave me a short nod. "A very brave boy."

"Did he have a name?" My voice was thick.

"Not that I know of, but you can still give him one."

Yes, I would give him one. "Can I summon him again?"

"I think you know the answer to that question," he said softly.

Even with sleep trying to drag me under, I could see the obvious. Magic no longer pulsed within the seed. It was just a seed now. I closed my palm, promising myself that I'd plant "Marvel" in my *Santa's Little Helper* pot. He'd get the love and attention he deserved.

My eyelids grew unbearably heavy. Light from the sunrise warmed my face, yet I couldn't shake the chill that passed through me. I surrendered and closed my eyes.

I caught the scrapes of Nick's chair scooting closer. He took my hand and squeezed, spreading his warmth to Marvel and me.

"Will you be here when I wake up?" I asked.

"Yes."

"You…promise."

"Always."

**D**reams, even ones induced by wizards, tended to be strange affairs. Either I danced among the clouds or roller-skated down trippy, rainbow spray-painted roads. This time a woman waited for me beside a stream.

"Where are my hounds?" she demanded.

I stopped cold. I tried to make myself wake up but couldn't.

"Don't make me repeat myself, *human* or I'll strike you dead in your sleep." Her dark gray eyes stormed and flashed.

Somehow, I managed to speak. "They're gone. We sent them to a place where even I can't retrieve them."

Diana touched the hunting bow at her feet. Her quiver rested nearby. It was full of silver-tipped wooden arrows. "You think you've bested me, haven't you?"

She'd whispered those words, but the menace in her tone was far more frightening than a shout.

I crept backward, only to hit a wall of trees. "There's no winning against you," I said. "You're immortal."

She smirked. "But I've lost my hounds. And you've evaded me twice now."

I glanced around, finding nowhere to go. Either I stood my ground or gave up. A new feeling quaked in my stomach. It was small at first, then it grew until I couldn't stand still.

I'd had enough of her shit.

"What do you want?" This was my dream, after all.

"I want to hunt. I *must* win."

"You won't win this one—you can't. 'Cause I'm not afraid of you anymore. Come for me then." More strength surged through me. "I'll cross a thousand worlds to outmaneuver you again."

I began to walk away along the tree wall. Once I woke up, I had living to do.

The huntress rose, her face contorting into a vicious snarl. I turned to face her as the goddess's bow materialized in her hand. "How dare you turn your back on me."

Diana's eyes glinted with a cold determination as she plucked an arrow from her quiver. Her fingers danced over the feathered fletching with an unsettling grace. The moonlight gleamed off the razor-sharp tip. Diana notched an arrow and took aim. The sinister grin on her face widened as she advanced in my direction. The quiver on her back whispered with every step.

"The hunt ends now—" Diana's words were cut off as a thick fog swept in around us. The tranquil lake nearby stilled.

"Ugh…why can't you leave me be?" Diana said.

Three figures slipped out of the wavering fog: an old

woman, a middle-aged one, and a younger one. They were dressed in light blue robes.

"Enough, Diana," said the youngest one. "This one has a long thread, and you will not be the one to clip it."

"How dare you! You can't have your way this time—" Diana demanded.

"There is no *way*," the crone said. "Only the thread and the innocent lives weaved with it."

The maid added, "Your hunt for Natalya Stravinsky is over. Your father has caught wind of your behavior, and Zeus summoned us to intervene on his behalf. You must return to Olympus or face his wrath."

"And what if I refuse to go?" she demanded.

The maid smiled and retrieved a golden spool from her robe. "Then we shall do as ordered."

"You sneaky bitches." Diana shifted to aim in their direction, but the maid tossed the shiny, golden spool to the crone. The motion slammed Diana to the ground.

The Three Fates turned to me.

"This isn't for you to witness, Wolf," the crone said. "She Who Always Walks the Path must return to where she belongs. You must do the same."

"You're free now," the maid said. With a flick of her fingers, the fog swept in and swallowed me whole.

# CHAPTER TWENTY-FIVE

Aweek came and went. Each day crept painfully along as I rested in my parents' spare bedroom. Once I could stand on my own, Mom begrudgingly let me return home.

While I was gone, Thorn had moved everything back into the house. My keen-eyed mate had even placed everything exactly as I'd left it. Every box of holiday cheer was stacked in the living room with loving care and Marvel's pot had a place of honor on the kitchen windowsill. And that wasn't all. Pack members had stuffed our freezer with every lasagna imaginable and Will had mowed our lawn. Old Farley had even carved a welcome home gift: two little wooden wolf figurines for our fireplace mantel.

Home was truly home again.

So why did I wander from room to room like one of Quinton's zombies? This morning I'd even put on a pencil skirt and blouse. My old work uniform practically embraced me with open arms. Now that I didn't have a job anymore, I was cast adrift.

The day's monotony ended when my cell beeped with an

incoming message. I hurried to the phone like a junkie pining for a fix. It was from Bill. Was the goblin ready for me to return?

The message read: *I heard you're back home. Seemed like an ideal time to give you the good news. I sold the Ramneil. With the profits, I plan to improve The Bends for its employees.*

After reading the first part of the message, I grinned from ear to ear. Holy shit, that sneaky goblin—who I thought didn't have a single noble bone in body—had really come through for everyone. I wondered how much the pay raise would be. I squealed with joy until I read the rest of the message: *You'll be happy to know I had a delightful chat w/the new owner, the night demon. She didn't know you were done w/Diana so I told her you were free and clear! She said you two have unfinished business and you'll be hearing from her soon.*

That was it. No come back to work, no checking in to see if I was well. He'd sold me up the river. I typed out five—make that six—replies to Bill. Each one bordered on vindictive so I deleted them. Just once I wanted that goblin to do right by me.

Well, there went celebrating. At least my friends might get something out of the sale.

I thought I'd spend the day in pissed off silence, but someone knocked on my door not long after two in the afternoon. I could smell the bag of Cheetos she'd eaten long before she crossed my doorstep.

"Hey, Aggie!" I let her in. "What's up?"

My best friend carried two full grocery bags. She still wore her work uniform from Barney's, a pair of beige slacks and white T-shirt. "Did your mom tell you about the cookout tonight?"

Of course, Mom didn't. If someone would've spilled the details, I would've come up with an excuse to not go.

"Yeah, she told me," I lied.

Aggie cackled with glee as she headed to the kitchen. I hurried after her and eyed those bags. Aggie coming over only meant two things: she wanted to catch up and she planned to use my double ovens in the process.

I sighed and tried to think of an excuse. Since I couldn't lie, I mumbled, "What do you need?"

Since I didn't have much to do, other than recover, I scrubbed down the house. Memories of the first time she'd helped herself to my home, back when I wasn't the alpha female, came to mind. At the time, I'd entered my kitchen to find Julia Child baking her heart out in my once-clean kitchen.

"Are you making pineapple upside down cakes again?" I asked.

Last time she'd left flour all over the floor, spilled pineapple on the counters, and she hadn't bothered to clean the soiled spoons and bowls as she worked. The greatest crime she'd committed was leaving the broken eggs *in* the carton, but I refused to go there.

"I've moved on. Those are easy," Aggie said. "I'm caught up on all the seasons of *The Great British Bake Off*, so I wanna do something cool like old-fashioned picnic pies."

The term "old-fashioned" set off alarm bells in my head, but the clangs were immediately silenced when Aggie deposited her things on the counter and swooped in to give me a hug.

"I missed you, Nat," she said softly.

I rested my head against her shoulder. She was the perfect height for hugs. "I've missed you too."

She let me go and said, "And don't worry about the mess I'm about to make. I promise I'll clean up before I leave."

"I don't mind." I actually meant what I'd said and it felt good.

Aggie unpacked her ingredients. "Even if you don't, rest assured, I'm certified now."

"Certified?"

Her blue eyes brightened. "I'm a certified food service professional now." She placed a pack of raw hamburger into the fridge. "After working at Barney's in a management role, I've had a lot of time to think about what I'd like to do with my life."

I chuckled. "The service industry is a great place to question your life goals."

"I happen to love it and there's been *developments* too." She rifled through my cabinets until she found my bright red pastry mixer.

"Do tell." I settled on a nearby kitchen seat.

"Barney's owner wants to move overseas in December, and he asked me if I'd be interested in taking over." She bit her lower lip. "I think I'm gonna say yes."

My mouth dropped. "A franchise is a huge responsibility."

"I'm gonna owe half a mil to the bank, but I'm excited." She shrugged. "My dad wanted me to work for him way back when. It'd be nice if I could do the same for myself."

"You will," I said firmly.

She paused and grinned. "You and I have come a long way."

I couldn't resist smiling, but I did feel a bit jealous. I didn't want to own a restaurant, but who didn't dream of making something for themselves?

"Oh my God, yes." Aggie shook her head. "I'm glad you didn't kick me out when I tried to sneak into your old place."

That was a special night. I'd been alone and fearful, but Aggie had showed up—like today—and she'd yanked me out of my foul mood.

Aggie arranged the ingredients to prepare the hot water

crust pastry. She hummed and presented her back to me while she worked. Her ponytail flopped back and forth.

"You're about to own a business, you've got your own apartment." While she worked, I fetched some mini pie tins from my pantry. "Are you about the save the world?"

"I wish." She twisted to reveal her relaxed expression. "What I do know is I need help too. With the overeating stuff."

We rarely discussed Aggie's habit of overeating. I never pried too much since I had my own problems.

"Are you ready for therapy again?" I asked.

"I think I'm *more* than ready." Her hands slowly kneaded the dough. "I've had long conversations with Brenna and Erica about my mental health."

For a moment, I wondered why she hadn't confided in me, but then I considered the listener. Brenna had medical training and quite the mellow mood. Erica got to the point. They'd enriched her life—just like me.

I glanced at the clock and noted how much Aggie needed to do to finish her picnic pies. As much as I didn't want to attend the cookout, I wanted to help Aggie present her best self—through the food she enjoyed so much. I washed my hands to help.

Even with her atrocious cooking habits, Aggie would also be there for me. We'd weaved in and out of each other's lives, but what always remained was how we had each other's backs. I wouldn't let her fail and it was a comfort to know she'd do the same for me.

# CHAPTER TWENTY-SIX

After a long morning baking with Aggie, Thorn and I drove over to the park. Not a single cloud dotted the sky—it was a perfect day for fellowship and food.

Familiar cars and trucks filled the parking lot, and I spied several parties unloading their food. To my delight, Oswald from Gray Folk Feathers, as well as Esmeralda and her uncle, from the Brownie Baking Company, had decided to come. They nodded my way.

South Toms River Pack members were in attendance too. Erica and Aggie waved at me from one of the many picnic tables surrounding the main white gazebo. Folks chatted and ate while children played with water balloons. Six of my older cousins were in the middle of playing football.

The sweet scent of roasted beef wafted past my nose. Mom must've gotten up early to arrange such a grand feast. My family had already lined up the fixings on the main tables underneath the gazebo. Pack members lined up for a plate by hierarchy. As werewolves, you couldn't escape the pecking order, even when you wanted some chow.

I walked over to greet Grandma. She sat in a place of honor next to Farley at the largest table under the gazebo. I nodded to Farley and took in Grandma. Today she wore a brand-new, knee-length dress. That had to be one of Aunt Olga's. The garment had a lovely peach print with sprinkles of pineapples. Usually, Grandma would never be caught in such a thing, but she appeared spry today with her hair free from a scarf and her smile wide for the world to see. When she spotted me, she opened her arms.

After I kissed her cheeks, she said, "You're late."

"We're right on time," Thorn said in broken Russian.

Grandma beamed. "Not bad, my boy."

"It took me forever to whip up a dish to bring," I admitted.

Grandma's gaze flicked to the sad-looking potato salad I held. Even her nose could tell I'd emptied a package from the store and dumped it into the bowl.

Aunt Olga and Aunt Vera walked over to greet me. We exchanged hugs before Aunt Olga stole my bowl away.

"I'll find a *place* for this on the table," she said. Based on the disapproving look she gave Aunt Vera, Aunt Olga meant that bowl would *never* be seen again.

Before I could chat more with Grandma, other pack members, like Jake and Misty from Archie's Burgers, lined up to greet me. A few of my friends couldn't wait to sneak in a quick hug.

It was so damn good to stand here and just be normal.

After a brief chat with a couple folks, Thorn managed to pull me away to come eat. Just sitting at the main table in the gazebo should've set my mind at ease, but I couldn't help missing the folks who weren't here. I stirred the food around my plate before I got a stern eye from Grandma to eat. Before I scooped the food into my mouth, I couldn't believe the couple who walked up to join us.

"Uncle Boris!" I abandoned my food to run to my uncle and Calliope. The pair appeared well. Calliope wore her usual jeans and T-shirt, while Uncle Boris was dressed in a Hawaiian T-shirt and khaki pants.

When I hugged him, I noticed he'd swapped his god-awful aftershave for some Old Spice. Perhaps the elf had chosen another one for him. *Good choice, my dear.*

Thorn beckoned them to join us at the main table. While we walked over, I couldn't resist asking questions.

"When Dad told me he'd gotten a hold of you, I couldn't believe it. Where have you two been all this time?" I asked.

Calliope took a seat while Uncle Boris scurried over to the food table. He grabbed not one, but two plates. I grinned. He'd become quite the doting boyfriend, I tell you.

"We've been traveling," Calliope said. "The fae have hired me to kill for many years, so it was nice to simply relax for a while."

Uncle Boris returned to the table with some drinks and the food. The two plates were piled high with hamburgers, hotdogs, and a generous serving of my mother's *olivie*, or Russian potato salad. To my genuine surprise, the fairy dug into the Russian food with gusto. Most of my human friends didn't care for it.

My aunts looked on and nodded with approval.

"It was rough when the hellhound showed up," Uncle Boris said. "But my lady here had a plan. She told me if those puppies liked running in circles, then we'd tire them out."

"How did you get them to chase you?" Thorn asked.

Uncle Boris gave a full-bellied laugh and took a swig of his Budweiser beer. "When we'd first threw the hounds off Natalya's trail, we'd used her clothes. Since I didn't have any, I had to get creative."

Other pack members quieted to hear the story.

Uncle Boris continued. "You see, scents are everywhere.

Back in World War II, whenever I wanted to find someone at the barracks, I tracked them from their bed."

"Rather clever, Boris," Aunt Vera said. "So you used Natalya's bedspread."

The couple had their mouths full, so they nodded at the same time. It was rather cute.

My father added, "They managed to keep the hellhounds busy for five hours. Can you believe it?"

Mom and her sisters laughed with glee.

Uncle Boris finish chewing and added, "We had to give up when we ran out of gas. I had to convince Callie to turn and run."

"Who runs from a fight?" Calliope's mouth was full, and yet her voice carried through the gazebo.

Pack members cheered and I laughed. Uncle Boris's woman would fit in just fine.

"What are your plans?" Aunt Vera asked Uncle Boris.

Uncle Boris wiped off his mouth and he stole a glance at Calliope. "My lady and I will travel some more."

"You're leaving us for good?" Aunt Vera asked, and others echoed her question.

"What about your job?" Mom pushed me farther down the table to sit next to him.

Thorn shook his head in amusement and kept eating.

"A job is a job," Uncle Boris said softly. "But I've been lonely for a very long time."

With all the women Uncle Boris had dated, he was rarely alone, but now that I thought about it, he'd been looking for love. For true companionship.

"When are you leaving? Thorn asked.

"We'll leave in a couple months. I need to finalize some things," Uncle Boris said as he wrapped his arm around Calliope's shoulder.

With the Stravinskys back together, even if only for a

couple of months, I couldn't help but let my gaze sweep over my precious family. Now that I was free from Diana, Thorn and I could travel, maybe even start a family. The thought left me giddy with excitement, yet apprehensive about the challenges to come.

Speaking of pups, Sveta had escaped from Karey and now she wandered from adult to adult with her mouth open wide for food. When she reached me, she wanted to get picked up instead. As I drew her close and ran my nose along the sweet spot on her forehead, I knew that when the time came, I'd be ready.

Overtime, the crowd at the park shrunk and grew as more friends and family stopped by. Even my friends from group therapy stopped by. Tyler had rented a car and everyone had stuffed themselves inside, but there was one person I was hoping to see one more time before he disappeared down the rabbit hole in New York City.

The man in question popped up less than an hour later. Brenna and Nick appeared hand in hand from the forest. Brenna donned a white sundress while Nick wore his usual goth garments, minus his *coat*.

My mouth dropped.

Hell had officially frozen over and the damned were ice skating in the fields.

I stole a glance at Aggie and we shared a girlish giggle.

"Is that what I think it is?" I asked her.

"Looks like Nick is finally getting comfortable with Brenna."

Pack members swooped in to greet them warmly. The white wizard and the earth witch were given two seats of honor at the main table. Nick sat next to me, while Brenna took the spot on his other side.

"Thanks for coming, Nick," I said.

"I wouldn't have missed it," he replied said with a smile.

"Brenna kept saying we'd have to show up, or the Stravinskys would roll up to New York to find us."

"We've much to celebrate," my dad said from the other side of the table. "My daughter's free from Diana and you're one of the many souls I wish to thank."

Other pack members nodded. Before Nick and Brenna could refuse a meal, the Stravinsky women placed generous plates of food before them.

"We just came to say hello and hang out." Nick eyed the pile of food on the paper plate.

Not a single person had washed their hands or wiped off the table from the last person who'd eaten at his spot.

"I happen to be hungry," Brenna said. She pushed the meat aside and dug into the vegetables.

"You don't have to eat," I whispered to Nick.

Thorn offered him an unopened bottle of sweet tea and Nick accepted it with a grateful nod.

"How you holding up?" Thorn asked Nick.

"Good." For once, Nick sat among friends without his shield—his black trench coat and fedora hat. He took a drink of his tea, and I even spied a sheen of sweat forming on his brow. "Been a long morning."

The two men made small talk about the upcoming base-ball game between the Yankees and the Mets. Their conversation stretched out, and yet the sweat gathering on Nick's neck, shoulders, and chest. Was he really that hot…or was something else going on?

A couple minutes later, I finally touched the top of his hand. "You okay?"

His mouth opened and closed like a dying fish. "There's something I wanted to do when we got here, but now I don't know what to do," he whispered.

I gave him a smile. "You made it here, Fenton and you're amongst your friends. It's okay to just *be*."

He drew a deep breath. "Just be…"

To my surprise, Nick got up and stood behind Brenna. He reached into a pocket of his jeans and withdrew a tiny golden box.

A couple heads turned toward the gazebo. Whispers erupted when Nick bent down on one knee and extended the golden box toward Brenna. She turned around to face him when she noticed everyone else had quieted and many mouths had dropped open.

"Nick…" she breathed. "What are you doing?"

Nick briefly closed his eyes before he said, "Brenna Bourdon, will you honor my family and my name by marrying me?"

Aggie squealed while an astonished Brenna sat there.

The earth witch's lower lip began to tremble. "Yes, Nicolas Fenton. I will honor you and your family, and I will marry you."

Whoops and hollers started in the gazebo, then spread to the other tables. The cheers grew louder when Nick opened the box, revealing a breathtaking gold ring with emeralds. While putting it on her finger, he fumbled a couple times.

"Don't drop it, boy," Uncle Boris said with a chuckle.

"I won't." Nick's right hand wouldn't stop shaking so he grasped it with his left.

"I never thought he'd ever ask," Brenna wiped away a tear. "I didn't expect this."

"Finding love is the best kind of surprise." I stole a glance at Thorn and he winked at me.

Now that my welcome home cookout had turned into an engagement party, the mood lifted even higher. Mom turned on some Russian pop music and the more inebriated family members danced. Aggie and Erica got up to bust a move. I tried to watch, but when Aggie shuffled over to get me to join, I didn't want to give up Sveta.

My little darling had dozed off, and like all aunties, I wanted to spoil her as long as possible. And well, nobody needed to see my horrible dance moves. I settled into the seat and my gaze swept over my family, new and old. Life was good.

My phone buzzed in my pocket and something told me not to check it. So far, I'd received congratulatory messages from my family in Russia, but a tickle on the back of my neck sounded off in warning. If it was my cousin Yuri though, I'd feel bad.

I whipped out my phone to see a message from an unknown name: *You and I still have unfinished business, Natalya. Come to Ramneil Pawn & Market tomorrow at sunset.*

The demon had finally called in her debt.

# CHAPTER TWENTY-SEVEN

With the night demon's text message weighing down the phone in my pocket, I headed to Ramneil Pawn & Market the next evening. I had to park in the shared lot next to The Bends. It almost felt like a crime to amble over to the other building.

The inside of the empty store was just as decrepit as I'd remembered it. The place had closed over a month ago and not much had changed. After the attack on The Bends, most of the supplies in here had been used to constrain Wilhelm. Now they were stacked and crammed haphazardly into any nook or cranny. The very idea that I'd have to somehow bring all this together as a new store for the undead and any wandering spirits up the Parkway left me baffled.

"What do you think of the place?" The midnight demon stood behind me, making an unexpected appearance as usual.

"What are we doing here?" I asked. "I thought you wanted to talk about my debt."

She ignored my question. "This store has good bones."

"Good bones on a corpse, if you asked me."

"There is a lot of potential in this location, even without Diana's supernatural influence." She strode around me toward the center of the cavernous room.

Now that Diana no longer hunted nearby, the supernatural creatures drawn to her presence would go away, but the humans and their cold cash would remain. And I preferred boring humans any day.

"I can see why Bill set up shop in town, all those years ago," the night demon said. "I prefer the river side, to be honest."

"You do have a boat. Don't you need to be close to the water?"

"For some of my customers, yes. My sister likes the water too."

We grew quiet for a bit and I took in her face. What was the night demon hiding from me? Did she sell me off to someone else?

The building yawned, not from magic, but from an oncoming summer shower. My whole body was weary, but work was work and if I had made this place happen, I'd put one hundred percent into it.

I stood straighter and asked, "Should I come back to tonight or tomorrow to clean up?"

Mademoiselle Midnight glanced me, and the starlight in her hair briefly flared like a supernova. "Yes…I do need to finalize things."

My gaze swept over the furniture. Maybe we could save a couple displays. Some of them would need to be drop-kicked like a bad habit into a dumpster. Trashing them might feel good.

Mademoiselle Midnight spoke again. "The offer to buy the place from Bill was impossible to resist. Who wouldn't want an opportunity to one-up a goblin like him. And I must admit, you were one of the best employees I ever had."

Good employee or not, I didn't want to be here. "I'll sort out the trash then."

Her grin widened. "I was prepared to move here and setup shop, but then I had a visitor a couple days ago."

I faced the midnight demon and tried to hide my shock.

"It was your grandmother," the madame said. "We had the most delightful conversation until I had to rest for the day. She listens and speaks well."

I nodded as the madame continued. "She told me about her family. In particular, her siblings who were long gone. She described them so well—I could see their faces and even imagine their voices. And her aunt Lada! Now, she was quite the spunky thing. Back then was so different before modern machines and the Internet. We spent time with people. We cherished them. Now we exist until those who are most precious to us are taken away." She sighed and the smoke trailing from her peplum shirt shimmered from white to soft chartreuse. "Not long after Svetlana and I chatted, I realized I couldn't stay in South Toms River. My place should be with my sister."

Fear pricked my spine. I took a step back. Did that mean I had to go north with her?

"What about the shop?" I dared to ask.

She gave me a coy smile.

"I think I know someone," she said. "She'd make a great owner."

"Excuse me? Did you say *owner*? How would I own this place when I owe *you* the debt?" That demon had lost her mind. I'd taken her jade beads, swallowed them like M&M's, then I never saw them again.

"There are some things that are more valuable than money in this world. It's time. My place is to wander the Earth with my sister for all time. Your place is here, not bounced back-and-forth from shop to shop to pay your debts. You'll make it your own, and with that, you can move forward into the *future*."

The words "Are you sure?" came to mind, but only a fool would say such things. I'd never imagined saving up to own my own place. I thought I'd work at The Bends until I was grandma's age. That place, including Bill, Erica, Quinton, and everyone else, were just as much a part of me as my family. And yet as I walked away from the night demon to survey the room, the possibilities of what I could do here left me heady—almost as excited as the day I had returned home from my first day at The Bends of the River Flea Market.

"Is it a yes?" the night demon asked.

I didn't hesitate. "With those kinds of terms, I think it is."

"What do you plan to sell here?" Her eyes twinkled with mischief. "You're not going to put me out of business, are you?"

"Maybe." My heart swelled with joy at the possibilities. "I think I should sell hope. We all need a lot more of that these days."

The End

# PRAISE FOR SHAWNTELLE MADISON

A smart, sexy, rip-roaring good time!

ANGIE FOX, NYT BESTSELLING AUTHOR

Coveted is odd, funny, original and not at all what you'd expect. The writing is excellent, the characters come off so realistic they should have their own reality show, and the story is authentic and original.

LYNN VIEHL, NYT BESTSELLING AUTHOR

Characters of all shapes, sizes and species abound in this new series from debut author Madison...How can you go wrong when your heroine is a werewolf with OCD? Madison tells her story with a lot of humor, and readers will be waiting with bated breath for her next story.

ROMANTIC TIMES BOOK REVIEWS

This is the start of a funny and touching new paranormal series, which may be dealing with supernatural creatures, but gives them all very human problems that make them very relatable. I loved this book and can't wait to see what's in store for Natalya next!

PARKERSBURG NEWS AND SENTINEL

# COVETED

"*A regular person in a magical body, Natalya's struggles with her job (irritable Harpies trying to return vases!) and love life are both hilarious and heartwarming.*"

—NYT Bestselling Author Eloisa James
Reading Romance Column
B&N Review

Prequel
Novella
0.5

Book
1

Book
2

Novella
2.5

Book
3

Short Story
Collection

Prequel feat.
Aggie
McClure

VALKYRIE
RISING
PRESS

# ABOUT THE AUTHOR

**Shawntelle Madison** is a Web developer who loves to weave words as well as code. She'd be reluctant to admit it, but if pressed, she'd say that she covets and collects source code. After losing her first summer job detasseling corn, Madison performed various jobs, from fast-food clerk to grunt programmer to university webmaster. Writing eccentric characters is her favorite job of all. On any given day when she's not surgically attached to her computer, she can be found watching cheesy horror movies or the latest action-packed anime. Shawntelle Madison lives in Missouri.